A SINFUL CLASSROOM

A STUDY HARD ROMANCE

MIKA LANE

HEADLANDS PUBLISHING

COPYRIGHT

BE THE FIRST TO KNOW...

Want more heat, heart,
and bad boys who know what they're doing?
Join my list and I'll send the steam straight to your inbox,
starting with a deliciously naughty story:

SIGN UP TO MY MAILING LIST!
Or visit:
https://geni.us/free-book-signup

1

ROXY VANDENBERG

"I'm not on the class roster?"

My calculus professor sighed, like mine was the most difficult question she'd been asked all day, which was unlikely, considering she taught the miserable subject of differential equations. She rotated the piece of paper resting between us, her class roster, so I might take a look at the undeniable evidence, proof that I was indeed *not* signed up for her class.

I scanned her alphabetical class list as if my name might magically appear. As I did, Professor Bitch held the paper in the tense grip of her forefinger and thumb, like I might try to snatch it and run away.

What kind of students was she used to dealing with?

"As you can see," she huffed, "there is no one on my list named Roxy Vandenberg."

She spat my name like it tasted bad.

Miserable woman. But I guess I'd hate my life too if

5

I taught calculus and its more horrible offspring, known as 'differential equations.'

"I don't understand" I said as the rest of the class brushed past, stampeding out the door. "I've got to be there. I registered at the end of last semester, like I did all my other classes."

Behind her, I watched the rest of the class leave as quickly as they could, further evidence that no one wanted to take her dreadful subject. I would bet my life that every last person enrolled was there only because they *had* to be. Like some sicko curriculum designer had decided that business majors, like me, needed calculus.

Sadists, all of them.

She snatched the class list back, returning it to her folder of other Important Papers.

"I know I'm signed up," I pressed. "I even got a confirmation that I was in. It must be some sort of mistake that I'm not on your list."

As much as the subject turned my stomach, I needed this stupid class. And, as much as she wanted to brush me off, I wasn't going away before I was ready.

She looked at her watch, the universal sign for *I'm done here*, and shrugged. "I'd check with the registrar's office if I were you," she said, and turned on her heel.

Ouch.

I was tempted to say, in my best you-are-a-horrible-person tone, that while she might believe otherwise, no one—and I mean *no one*—wanted to take her class, *ever*. There was no world in which someone looked forward to calculus or its unfortunate little cousin nicknamed 'diffy-q's.'

That would hit her where it hurt, no doubt.

But I kept my big mouth shut. If she didn't know by now that calculus was voted the course from hell at Wellshire University, well, I'd happily clue her in another day.

But I had shit to take care of right now.

It was funny, though. On my way to class, just sixty minutes earlier, I'd been psyching myself up for the subject. Hell, if every other student in my department had managed to pass it, then of course I could, too. My optimism had even put a little spring in my step as I hustled through the campus's freezing wind tunnel, wishing I had a warmer winter jacket.

Actually, I'd *had* a heavier jacket, but passed it on to my younger sister. I figured she needed it more than I did, and I'd told myself I'd be fine with the old cloth coat my mother handed down to me. But the mid-winter gale-force winds blustering through campus said otherwise.

How stupid was I? I'd been at Wellshire for three years now. I knew how cold the place got in the winter.

"Vandenberg. Roxy Vandenberg," an officious voice called over the registrar's office loudspeaker when my turn came.

I jumped to my feet and pushed through the crowd of students trying to get their schedules straightened out on the first day of the semester.

Did they all have the same issue I did?

"Um, hi," I said to the slack-faced clerk. "My name wasn't on the roster of my first class today, so I thought I'd stop by to see what was up—"

"Name and social security number please," she barked without looking at me.

Fuck, I hated being interrupted. But I was in no position to provide this stranger the lesson on manners she needed. First things first.

"Here is my identification, Miss... um, what was your name?"

She ignored my request, just typing my information into her computer at breakneck speed. After a minute, she looked back at me, frowning. "Your tuition bill is unpaid," she said with a sigh, like she told people that all day long.

Maybe she did. Paying for college wasn't easy. Unless you had well-off parents, which I did not. But that didn't make me any less worthy of her respect. It wasn't like I was some sort of freeloading slacker, trying to game my way through college without paying. I'd come up with my tuition money for the last six semesters. You'd think that counted for something.

I tapped my foot to bleed off frustration, but she backed away from the plexiglass window separating us, anyway. I'd never been too good at hiding my emotions. But I was trying that day. It wouldn't pay to take my shit out on a paper-pusher.

I forced a lame smile. "Can you check again please? Because I think that's a mistake," I asked, politely but firmly gesturing at her computer, like it was the machine's mistake and not hers. Because of course.

She clicked around her keyboard, read the screen for another minute or more, and looked back at me. "I can only tell you what the system is telling me. If your bill is unpaid, your name is not provided to any of the professors. You don't show up on the class rosters. You need to see what's up with your bill at the bursar's office. They can tell you more. I only deal with class registration."

She turned her computer screen so I could see it. Sure enough, next to my name was a big red onscreen 'UNPAID' glaring back at me, mocking all my academic and life ambitions, like the ugly word that it was.

Complete and total bullshit.

"Um, thanks," I muttered, completely insincerely, shoulder-chucking my way through the crowd to get out of there.

I hiked two floors down to the bursar's office, where I pulled a number for what looked to be another interminable wait. Just like in registration, the place was beyond crowded, so full there were at least twice as many students as there were chairs in the waiting area. In fact, there were so many people sitting on the floor a security guard had been called. Looked like there were a lot of students with scheduling *and* payment problems. I felt slightly better knowing I wasn't alone and had to wonder, was the university making *that* many mistakes with their records, as they had in my case, or were there just that many student deadbeats behind on their bills?

Either way, I was certain my issue, when we got to the bottom of it, would be resolved quickly.

But when my turn finally came, the news I got wasn't any better than what the registrar's clerk had given me.

In fact, it was multitudes worse.

"Ms. Vandenberg," my clerk shrilled with a gleeful and slightly elevated voice, I was pretty sure designed to attract attention, "your bill is unpaid. You must pay it before you can attend classes."

For fuck's sake.

I tried to swallow, but my throat was dry. "Right," I said, pausing to make sure I had her undivided attention. "That's what I was told at the registrar's office. And, that's why I'm here. The thing is, my bill *is* paid. There must be some sort of mix-up."

I smiled like everything would be fine. I was a believer in positive thinking.

But the clerk wasn't convinced. Instead, she just repeated herself, only more loudly.

Could I be kicked out of school for murdering a pencil-pushing bureaucrat?

But I knew to keep it together. This matter would be resolved simply. I needed to preserve my brain cells for the more challenging thinking that was going to be required for my calculus homework. There was clearly a simple mistake made somewhere, and I would get to the bottom of it.

"Well," I explained to the clerk, "you see, each semester I pay half my tuition and my parents pay the other half. We've both paid. I should be good to go."

After a couple clicks on her keyboard, she turned back to me. "Your balance is only *half* paid right now. That means one half is missing. And until you pay the other half, you can't attend classes. You are not allowed. In fact, you shouldn't even really be on campus."

She threw me possibly the most smug smile I'd ever seen, and in order to control myself, I clenched my fists until my nails cut my palms.

"Are you *sure* there are not two payments?" I asked, trying to head off the shrill tone my voice was starting to take on.

She glared at me without a modicum of compassion. "One payment was made at the end of last semester. There haven't been any others since."

No fucking way. It was not possible. I grabbed my phone to access online banking. I could at least confirm the school had gotten *my* payment.

I'd have to call Mom and Dad about the rest.

"But I'm sure my parents—" I started to say.

"You need to talk to them, Ms. Vandenberg. Until your account is paid in full, you are not considered enrolled. Would you like a refund for what you've paid so far? Or would you rather keep it as a credit for another time?"

No. Fucking. Way.

This was not happening. It was just not happening.

"Miss, are you okay?" she asked like she really cared. Which she clearly did not.

"Wh... why wasn't I informed? H... how did this happen?" I stuttered.

More keyboard clicks. "I see here a letter was sent to your home address a couple weeks back."

A letter? Was sent to my home?

Where one of my parents must have intercepted it.

But why? Why wouldn't they have told me about it?

While I stood there with rapid-fire questions shooting through my mind, the clerk looked past me, her face covered in impatience.

"Next," she called, as if I weren't there.

I wished I weren't there, either.

"You guys. The strangest thing just happened."

After calling my parents and getting their voicemail, I'd stumbled back to Birdie and Jessa's dorm from the admin building, not really seeing or hearing anything around me. In fact, I was pretty sure someone called out my name to say hi. But I couldn't make myself turn around to see who it was.

I felt like a zombie, lumbering along, unable to react to anyone or anything around me.

I spilled my story to my best friends, repeating myself at least three times because I just couldn't believe it.

"How could the school make such a stupid mistake? I mean, this is important shit. I could miss valuable classroom time that I may never be able to catch up on. All because of what is probably an accounting error."

My girlfriends nodded, occasionally looking at each other while I rambled, waiting for me to finish.

"What?" I asked, looking back and forth between them. "What's that look about?" I asked, breathless from non-stop talking.

Birdie, sitting on the edge of her dormitory-issued twin bed, propped her elbows on her knees, settling her chin in her hands.

Jessa, sprawled on her bed, studied her paint-stained cuticles, remnants of one of her art classes. I was pretty sure she was avoiding looking at me altogether.

I shifted uncomfortably in the desk chair I'd grabbed the moment I'd walked in. These girls were my posse. No two ways about it. But at the moment, I wasn't so sure they were on my side.

Jessa finally looked my way. "Roxy. There were signs this was coming," she said quietly.

"What? What was coming? What do you mean?"

Birdie opened her mouth to say something, then clamped it shut.

What the fucking fuck?

"*What?*" I shrilled at them.

"Roxy," she said slowly, "you know you paid *your* half of the tuition, so that means your parents didn't pay their half."

Yeah. Okay. *No.*

It was a mistake. I was sure of it.

She continued. "It's… not really that surprising. Your dad's car was repossessed last year, right? And didn't he pay your tuition late last semester, too?"

Well. Yeah. Dad was having some cash flow issues. But it all worked out. They'd eventually gotten the car back. How, I wasn't sure. But they had. And he paid my tuition on the first day of classes. If the university called that *late,* well then they could shove it up their asses.

But those were *signs*? Signs that should have told me something? Signs I should have done something about?

Fine. Dad wasn't the best with money. Neither was Mom. I mean, they didn't have much, what with Dad being a sub-subcontractor for a local construction company. They'd scraped by for years. But when he became a *subcontractor*, no longer two levels removed from the construction firm, things started looking up. We got better health insurance. And dental. Things changed at home—there was less tension and more laughter. We knew money wasn't everything, but having enough to cover the day-to-day sure felt good. My parents set aside what they could for my and my little sister's college. I still had to make up the differ-ence by working my butt off over the summer and during the school year, but the Vandenberg family was in good shape.

Not great. But good.

At least, I'd thought so.

"I hate to see you in this situation, but we want you to have open eyes. Ya know?" Jessa said.

Birdie nodded solemnly.

Open eyes? Open to what? What were they saying?

They didn't understand. They each had multiple dudes who worshipped the ground they walked on, who supported them in any number of ways. They didn't have a goddamn problem in the world.

They weren't *me*.

"What did your parents say?" Jessa asked hopefully.

"They didn't pick up when I called."

And now I was glad they hadn't. I was scared of what I might find out.

College was everything to me. If all went according to plan, I'd be the first in my family to graduate. I could break the cycle of living hand to mouth that I'd grown up with, the stress of which was a heavy burden. No one could know what it was like unless they'd lived it.

I would live in a better neighborhood. Even take my parents and my sister with me. I'd hold my head up everywhere I went, and when people asked me where I'd gone to college, I'd proudly say *Wellshire*.

Oh, great school, they'd respond with admiration.

The Vandenberg family was moving up in the world.

Suddenly, I wasn't so sure.

"Roxy, I could borrow some money from my parents—" Jessa started to say.

I held my hand up. "No. No way."

Her hurt expression told me to backpedal a little. "I

mean, thank you. Of course, I appreciate it. I know you want to help. But I couldn't accept that."

The offer was kind and made with the best intentions, I knew, but I chafed at the expressions on their faces. I didn't want sympathy. I didn't want pity.

Yeah, I was proud. So what?

"I… I might have to drop out. At least for a semester."

There. I'd said it. That was the absolute worst that could happen, and if it did, I'd survive. College wasn't going anywhere. I'd get back to it as soon as I could.

But it would break my fucking heart.

Birdie waved her hands around in a panic. "Wait, wait, wait. *No.* Don't you even consider leaving school. At least not yet. Go talk to your advisor. They know how to handle shit like this. They know how to navigate the university's resources. There is help for when people get in a bind. I know there is."

Fucking A. She was right. Even if those creeps in registration and the bursar's office couldn't be bothered to help me, there were others who could. I just had to figure out who.

I got to my feet.

"Look, Roxy," Jessa said. "Birdie and I hardly ever stay here in the dorm. We're always with the guys. So the room is yours while you get things sorted out. You know, if you're not wanting to go home. No one in the dorm will ask anything. They know who you are, you're here so much."

That's when tears filled my eyes and the lump grew

in my throat. But I wasn't going to cry. I stuffed those feelings right back down inside. I'd have my pity party later.

"Thank you," I croaked, taking Jessa's keys. "I can't tell you what this means."

It was true. I couldn't. There were no words to thank people who had your back no matter what. I could only hope they knew how much I appreciated them because I didn't know what the hell else to say.

So before I burst into tears, I hugged them both and headed back out, where I dialed my parents' number again.

Still no answer.

Then, I called my Dad's cell, even though I knew it was his busy time of day, and that it was unlikely he'd pick up.

Again, no luck.

A tiny bit lighter on my feet than when I'd left, I headed back to the admin building where I would hopefully find my advisor. He'd know what to do with my situation, just like Birdie had said. That's what those guys got paid for.

After all, I couldn't be the first student to have this sort of problem.

Right?

2

BAIRD PRIESTLY

"But Mr. Priestly, it's not fair."

Holy fuck. This conversation *again*?

I leaned onto my desk toward the advisee who I was desperately trying to keep in school. He, however, was not helping matters with his partying and shit grades. I was trying to let him know, in the most constructive way possible, that I could not single-handedly keep him from being booted. He had to occasionally go to class and get at least a few passing grades if he wanted to stick around. Without that, all the tricks I had up my sleeve wouldn't make a damn bit of difference. And this bit of information seemed to come to him as a surprise.

His whining was wearing me down, though. I actually wished, just for a moment, that he'd get kicked out of Wellshire University. And that was a dangerous, shitty attitude for a guy like me to have, considering academic advisors are supposed to help students *stay* in school and not fall on their asses, like this kid was right now.

"Brett, it's pretty straightforward," I said, leaning forward on my desk, hoping he'd finally grasp the severity of the situation. "You know what 'cause and effect' means, right? Let me give you an example. You get lousy grades, you end up on academic probation. You're on AP long enough, and the university asks you to leave. That's how college works. There's really no wiggle room. Blaming your pot dealer roommate doesn't figure into the equation."

Especially because I suspected his 'pot dealer roommate' didn't really exist, and that Brett was pretty much one hundred percent the cause of all his own problems. Making him see that, though, was another challenge altogether.

Jesus, when I was his age, I would have killed for half the opportunities he and most of his classmates had. Students like Brett really had no fucking clue how good they had it. I tried not to be sour about it—life hands out opportunities and is rarely fair about it, but some of these students could appreciate at least a small amount the nice hand they'd been dealt. The small community college I'd attended when I was their age had one academic advisor for the entire student body. Getting an appointment with her was as likely as wrangling an audience with the president. Actually, it was probably easier to get a meeting with the president. And word had it, when you did, nothing came of it anyway. The woman wasn't empowered to make anything happen. She was more of a sympathetic ear than anything.

So I was mostly on my own when navigating the strange world of college. It wasn't easy. I had no role models. No one in my family had attended, so they couldn't offer support. But I figured out, by sheer force of will, to keep my head down and study my ass off. If I didn't, I'd be out without a second glance. I was on my own, as were all the other kids who were my classmates.

But here at Wellshire, there were services for the students. Academic advisors like me. Hell, the reason I'd wanted to become one to begin with was to give students the help I never got, and to make their college years go a little more smoothly than mine did.

Was I succeeding?

Some days I was not so sure.

And students like Brett, plain and simple, depressed the hell out of me. They had it all. Set up at a top university, paid for by Mom and Dad, with the best computers to do their homework on, outstanding professors to learn from, and the money for tutors when they needed them.

And yet.

There would always be a Brett. I had to remind myself of that. Someone who took for granted the treasure trove of opportunity right before them. Someone who would *almost* let it slip directly between his fingers before he pulled back, got his shit together, and decided to behave like the adult he supposedly was.

Sometimes it took getting kicked out and having a semester off to deal with humiliation and pissed off parents before you grew up a little. It wasn't the end of the world. Some students needed that kind of kick in the ass.

Was I envious? I supposed so. Was I bitter? Maybe. But I tried not to be. The universe was random in how it meted out advantages. Some people, like Brett, got everything. Some people, like me, got next to nothing. But life was what you made it. I'd gotten out of the circumstances I'd grown up in. I wanted to help others do the same.

As soon as Brett and his type stopped wasting my damn time.

I nearly jumped for joy at the sound of a knock on my office door. I was pretty well out of patience, listening to Brett moan about his self-imposed predicament. I needed to wrap up our meeting before I lost my temper and told him what I really thought about him, which would be dangerous.

After all, academic advisors were decidedly *not* paid to tell students they were total fucking slack-ass losers.

Brett's whining continued as I reached for my office door. Was that rude of me, to walk away when he was mid-sentence? Hell yeah. But it would have been even ruder to take him by the shoulders, shake him, and tell him to grow the fuck up.

You had to pick your poison.

"Hello."

The student before me, one I'd met with only once

before and whose name I couldn't for the life of me remember, looked over my shoulder and into my office. Seeing Brett there, she sighed and took a step back.

"Sorry, Mr. Priestly. Didn't know you were with someone. Can we set up a time for me to come back later?"

But I reached to shake her hand because god knew I wasn't letting her get away, not only because it was high time for Brett to hit the road but also because she was so quietly beautiful. Tall and thin with slightly messy, unstyled blonde hair. Her brief smile revealed an adorable gap between her front teeth, and she wore a baggy plaid flannel shirt and the blue jeans with holes that were all the rage.

Yeah, I was checking her out. I couldn't lie. I might have been a member of the administration of a prominent university, but I was also a goddamn human. I didn't leave my balls at home when I came to work in the morning.

"Miss…" I said, waiting for her to fill in the blank.

"Vandenberg. Roxy Vandenberg." She took my hand and looked over my shoulder again at Brett. "Really. I can come back. I should have made an appointment."

But I wasn't letting her get away. After my initial once over, I focused on her eyes. And there was something in them that was—I don't know—scared, maybe. Like she needed help. Or needed *something*.

I'd seen that before. I'd felt that before.

I'd been that person.

I pushed my door the rest of the way open, and gestured for Roxy to come in. My office was tiny, and there really wasn't room for more than two adults. I hoped Brett would take the hint.

But when he just sat there like the entitled shit that he was, I realized it was time to be more direct.

"Miss Vandenberg, Brett here was just leaving," I said, gesturing broadly toward him.

We looked expectantly at Brett, whose ass remained solidly planted in the chair facing my desk. Jesus, was he that clueless?

I stretched to shake his hand, just far enough out of reach that he had to get out of his chair and move toward the door—a trick I'd learned from another colleague. Surprise washed over his face at the abrupt end to our meeting. Students like him were so used to being accommodated, it never occurred to them that others had boundaries.

And at the moment, mine was screaming *get the fuck out of my office.*

As we shook, I patted him on the shoulder with my free hand. "Let me know how things go, Brett."

That's when I realized he'd not gotten out of his chair to shake hands or even vacate my office like I so desperately wanted him to, but to get closer to my visitor.

He stood before her and smiled a smile that had probably been getting him laid since he was old enough to have a hard-on.

He squared his shoulders and pushed his chest out

against his Wellshire hoodie, like a peacock preening for a mate. "Hey, I know you," he said with a seductive half smile.

Fuck me. Was he really doing this right here?

"Roxy, yeah. Aren't you in one of my classes? I swear I know you. Calculus, maybe?" he crooned, running a finger down her flannel-covered arm.

Her gaze darted between the two of us, and she jerked away from him.

"Really, dude?" she barked.

His head snapped back.

I bit my tongue so I didn't laugh out loud.

The pitch of his voice deepened as if that might help. "Hey, I was just trying to be friendly. Maybe we could study together some time. You know, calculus is gonna be a bitch. I could help you."

Her eyebrows rose. "Um. Yeah. Right. Well, I might not even *have* any classes to take this semester, if I don't get my shit straightened out. So back off. I'm in a *shitty* mood right now and don't want to hurt anyone."

Damn.

And then, as if on cue, her bottom lip wobbled. Her hand flew to cover her mouth, and her eyes overflowed with the tears I suspected had been close to the surface all along.

Followed by one very loud sob.

Brett jumped back like she had something contagious. "Jesus. What the fuck is wrong with you?" he grumbled, moving toward the door.

"Um, Brett—" I said, putting a hand on his shoulder.

But he wasn't done. "I was gonna ask you out but no fucking way, now," he mumbled, hitting the road like his ass was on fire.

I pushed the door closed behind him and would have kicked him for emphasis if it wouldn't have meant my job. I loved what I did. Really. But it was hard some days, dealing with the Bretts of the world, whom I had so little respect for.

"Miss Vandenberg, would you like to take a seat and tell me what's going on?"

Stupid question, but I had to start somewhere.

She looked down to hide her pretty, tear-stained face, rapidly becoming red and puffy, and shook her head in between the heaving of her shoulders.

I normally never touched female students except to shake hands with them, but whatever was going on for this one was so damn tragic, my compassion got the better of me.

I put my hands on her shoulders and directed her to sit. "Okay, okay. Grab a seat here and catch your breath. Then you can tell me what's going on."

But instead of moving, she looked up at me, her eyes blood-shot and nose runny, and threw herself into my arms, probably having taken my hands on her shoulders as an invitation to a hug. Or something.

Well, shit.

My hands landed on her upper back and I started patting gently, unsure what else to do, as she buried her head against my chest. After a long minute, her sobs began to subside.

It wasn't that I didn't want a beautiful woman in my arms. Not at all. It was just that I didn't want a beautiful *student* in my arms. It just didn't seem… wise.

"All right. Okay now," I soothed, directing her, again, toward the chair Brett had vacated. "Please have a seat here and we can get to the bottom of this."

She took the hint.

"Oh my god, I'm so sorry. I didn't mean to unload on you like that," she sniffed, blowing her nose on a ratty tissue she'd pulled out of her backpack. "I never cry. But today has been a… bitch, let me tell you. That creep was lucky I didn't take it out on him with my fist to his nose."

Note to self: do not piss this woman off.

"Take your time. I want to hear the whole story."

She sniffled a few more times, her breath was ragged, the way it was after a good, hard cry, and she took a big inhale, dropping her head back and staring up at my cobwebby ceiling.

"Can I call you Roxy?" I asked.

That seemed to snap her out of it. "Of course. Please."

I passed her the box of tissues I kept in my bottom right-hand drawer.

In my kind of work, I tended to distribute a lot of tissues.

"Oh, thank you," she said, grabbing one and responding with a big honking blow.

She took a deep, yoga-type of breath, and I'd be

damned if her lower lip didn't tremble again. This was going to be a long meeting.

Not that I minded.

"I… I went to my calculus class this morning and found out I wasn't on the roster. Then, I went to the registrar and bursar. I'm not enrolled because my tuition bill is unpaid."

A couple leftover tears dribbled down her face, which she wiped away with the back of her hand.

"Dammit," she said. "I *hate* crying."

I hated to see her cry. But I kept that to myself.

"I take it that came as a surprise," I said.

Please don't let this be another Brett. She knew college had to be *paid for*, didn't she?

God help me.

"Yeah. It was a big surprise. I have a call in to my parents, but it's pretty clear they never paid their half of my tuition bill. You see, our arrangement is that I pay half and they pay half. I had no idea they hadn't paid until I went to calculus and found I wasn't on the roster. I don't know what's going on, I haven't reached them yet, but I'm scared. Scared I might not be able to continue with school. The bursar's office even offered me a refund on the portion of tuition I'd paid and suggested I use it *next* semester."

This led to a new round of tears, during which she choked out a bit more information. "I don't know what to do. My friends told me to come and talk to you about it."

She looked at me and shrugged, forcing a sad smile that again showed off that adorable gap in her teeth.

I didn't know which was the worst part of my job, dealing with the spoiled, irresponsible Brett type of student, or students like Roxy, who had real, honest to god problems like money issues.

The Roxys of the student world broke my heart, in part because I was once pretty much just like them.

But I could help. I *would* help. If someone really wanted to be in school, they deserved to be.

She buried her face in her hands and I knew if I were to make any progress, I had to work fast, before she was incapable of speaking again.

"I think I… I think I need to just drop out…" she gasped.

No. Just no. Just fucking no.

"Roxy, there are resources to help students like you. I can't let you quit. We'll find a way to make things work. It's my job to connect you with all the university resources at our disposal. Okay?"

She looked up at me, nodding woefully.

I'd been in her shoes. *This* was the sort of shit that wasn't fair. Not Brett's whiny excuses about a pot-smoking roommate.

"Keep attending your classes. You can audit them until we get this straightened out."

With a few clicks of my keyboard, I pulled up her records. Lived at home. Business major. Decent grades. Nothing outstanding, but she seemed to be putting in the effort. Then, I checked out the process for auditing classes, and printed out the information.

"First, get in touch with your parents to see if there's any way they can help—"

Which I knew was probably unlikely at this point, but it was always worth checking. They'd have paid the tuition if they'd had the money. The university, with all its reminders, didn't let the important task of collecting tuition fees slip from anyone's mind.

"—and I'll speak to the people in the work-study office. Do you have a job right now?"

She got to her feet and slung her backpack over a shoulder. "Yeah. I'm a hotel maid."

"All right then. See if you can take on some more hours. Maybe we can help you raise the money you need to pay the balance of the tuition. It's too late in the semester for scholarships, but we'll figure something out."

She shrugged. "I don't really have the grades for scholarships anyway. Probably because I work so much." She laughed sadly.

Time to make shit happen. I hated to see her leave in the shape she was in, but I had a meeting to get to, and besides, I wanted to talk to some people about her situation. It might be a lot of work to get her back on track. The university didn't take kindly to students with unpaid bills. But it would be worth it. For Christ's sake, that was why I was doing the work I did. To help students like Roxy.

And it wasn't just because she was so fucking beautiful.

Honest.

3

ROXY VANDENBERG

"Whoa. Now there goes what I call a serious hottie."

I dove into the far recesses of housekeeping's storage cabinet to restock the cart my coworker Lolo and I shared as we cleaned hotel rooms.

"Ugh. We never have enough of this spray stuff," I grumbled, grabbing the last two bottles.

But Lolo and I had what we needed for our shift. The other maids would have to figure something out. I was in no mood to care.

"Look, look, did you see him?" she hissed. "The guy with the dirty-blond, shoulder-length hair? Over there. *Look.*"

I craned my neck toward the hotel lobby, but saw no one.

She sighed. "Eh. He's gone now. You're too slow."

"Whatever, Lo. We have work to do. Let's get moving before Barney sees us gabbing."

It wouldn't be the first time Barney had caught us gabbing, and it wouldn't be the last. Lolo was a talker. She was almost as good at gabbing as she was scouting out hot hotel guests.

She glared at me. "Too bad you missed him. I haven't seen anyone like that in ages."

"Well, where did he go?" I asked.

She pointed. "The main conference room. Must be here for some sort of meeting."

I looked one more time to make her happy, and we watched the hotel's well-heeled guests come and go with their matched luggage sets and satisfied smiles, like they truly belonged in the lush surroundings of the nicest hotel in town. Which I guessed they did.

When I'd started working there, way back in high school, I'd been intimidated to no end. I shook every time I used the hotel's service entrance and couldn't manage to look any of the hotel guests in the eye when we passed in the hallways. That sorry mindset rapidly evaporated though, as soon as I learned that rich people were just as—if not more so—sloppy as anybody else.

I couldn't explain why I'd expected the rooms of the hotel's guests would be as pristine as their public-facing images. I guess it was just the naïve thinking of a high school kid who'd hardly been anywhere, or hardly seen anything.

It was when I started cleaning their rooms that I realized underneath it all, we were pretty much the same.

Rich people were still slobs, just with more expensive things.

I'd been a hotel maid for more than five years. Full-time in the summers and part-time during the school year, with extra shifts picked up as my school schedule allowed, often at the sacrifice of my grades.

If I had a dollar for every pair of dirty underwear I'd picked up off the floors of the very expensive hotel rooms I cleaned, well, I could probably buy the damn place.

Like I'd said, the rich were slobs just like the rest of us. Toenail clippings, used condoms, and makeup-stained towels were part of my daily routine. And that wasn't even the gross stuff.

In my time as a maid, there'd even been a couple old fuckers who'd 'accidentally' walked out of the bathroom nude after we'd started cleaning their rooms.

We knew they lived for the shocked look on our faces.

They had no idea we lived for the laughs they gave us.

But we had our own weaknesses, too. Sometimes, we looked at the women's clothes hanging in the closets. It was there, in the hotel, that I'd touched cashmere and silk for the first time. Lolo had even once logged onto someone's password-free laptop. That was way too risky for me, but I can't say I didn't enjoy looking over her shoulder.

Once, while dusting, we flipped on a room's DVD player to find the last guests had not only made a porno, they'd also forgotten to take it home with them. This treasure we passed around among the appreciative hotel staff before turning it into management. Last I heard, they'd called the guests to see if they wanted their 'property' back.

Yeah. It was that kind of hotel. Leave your porn video behind? Don't worry, we'll save it for you! Even mail it to you for free!

I knocked on the first room of the day.

"Housekeeping!" I yelled.

Our manager, Barney, beseeched us not to yell. Unseemly and all that. But I'd walked in on guests who hadn't heard me enough times to know that the only way to not surprise someone was to announce your arrival *very loudly*.

And just as we'd hoped, there was no response.

Lolo swiped the master keycard through the room's slot, and with a small whirring sound, the lock clicked open. She poked her head in and yelled again.

"Housekeeping!"

We got to work.

We were supposed to spend only fifteen minutes per room, so we flew through our list of tasks, checking them off one by one. Just before leaving, I was closing closet doors that had been left open when I spied a thick, shaggy fur coat. Without thinking, I reached to touch the soft fur, and when I found it was as delicious as I'd thought it would be, stroked it again.

It reminded me of the fur coat my dad had won in

some work contest when I was a kid. He'd brought it home for my mom, who'd actually worn it quite a bit. For a while, anyway. But she'd eventually had to sell it to a friend during a difficult time when we were broke. I didn't know which was worse. That my father had brought home the coat to begin with, or that his poor money management had put Mom through the humiliation of having to sell it off to a friend who'd always admired it.

Leaving her to see her friend wear it every time they went anywhere.

My stomach churned as my own current, fucked-up situation bubbled to the surface.

No. Not now. Go the fuck away.

"Hey. C'mon, Roxy," Lolo called. "We're gonna fall behind."

Right. Right.

Don't fall behind.

We were passing through the lobby when Lolo gave me a sharp jab to the ribs with her elbow. "There he is again. The hottie."

I followed her gaze to the man she'd described earlier.

Holy shit.

It was Baird Priestly, my academic advisor. The one I'd just met with. Whom I'd cried my eyes out in front of.

I ducked behind a large potted plant. "Lolo. C'mon. We gotta go."

She stood there, watching Mr. Priestly, as if he might come over and talk to her.

"Lolo. C'mon," I hissed.

"What?" she asked. "Do you know him or something?"

Without answering, I put my head down and pushed our cart toward the elevators, but not before I glanced at the sign outside the meeting room he'd emerged from.

Boys Club Monthly Meeting

He was involved with the Boys Club? Jesus. Good-looking *and* into volunteerism.

"I know him, Lolo. He's my advisor at school."

She jogged to keep up. "Let's go say hi, then!" she suggested.

"No. No. Let's just go, I don't want to say hi. Not now."

She rolled her eyes and shrugged. I was pretty sure I'd just ruined her day.

"Mom. *Mom.* What is going on here?"

I jumped out of the car and raced across my front yard, stepping around and jumping over things that used to be *inside* my house.

That for some reason were now *outside* my house. On the front lawn. That I used to mow when I was a kid. And still did the occasional cartwheel on.

Mom, frantic, glanced at me while trying to grab items out of the arms of the burly men removing things from our house. But she was outnumbered, and besides, she couldn't pick up a dresser or mattress anyway, no matter how much she wanted to.

"That was a gift from my mother!" she screamed as our beat-up old sideboard was carried past us.

Who were these guys? Thieves? Did thieves come in the middle of the day with big vans and help themselves to your shit while you stood there screaming at them to stop? Where were the police?

"Roxy!" Mom screamed when she saw me standing there, mouth agape. "Help me!"

She pointed at a queen size mattress, and gestured for me to get on the other side of it to carry it back into the house.

What the fucking fuck?

Without thinking, I ran to the other side of it and between the two of us, we moved it two whole inches.

Wait. What was I doing?

"Mom, please. *Stop*. What is going on? Tell me."

She brought her hand up to cover her eyes and winced. "They're taking everything. Just everything," she wailed.

Who were *they*? And why were they taking our things?

I grabbed my mom by the upper arms. "Why, Mom? What's happening?"

"It's… it's something your father has done. Something illegal. And now the government is seizing our property."

What? That made no sense. Dad was a construction subcontractor. He didn't do illegal things.

And could the government just come and take your stuff, anyway?

I looked around long enough to take in not only the huge moving van parked in the street, but also the string of neighbors lined up along the curb watching the freakshow that was my family's crisis. Some of them looked concerned. Others were enjoying themselves. No one was coming over to offer help.

That's when my father emerged from the house, head down, walking very fast.

"Dad!" I screamed, running to him.

He'd have some answers about what was going on, as well as what the hell had happened with my tuition.

"Not now, Roxy," he barked, trying to dodge me.

Um, don't think so, Dad.

"Tell me what's going on right now," I demanded, stepping in front of him.

But even as the words left my mouth, I knew there was a part of me that didn't want to know, because it was most likely linked to the non-payment of my tuition.

And if I'd thought I had a problem *before* I arrived at

my parents' house, well that shit had just been child's play.

Government officials?

Seizing property?

This was big-time fucked up.

Dad stopped long enough to look me in the eye. "I made some mistakes, Roxy honey. Bad mistakes. And now we all have to pay for it."

No fucking shit, Dad.

Then he stepped around me, managed to dodge my crying mother, got into a cab that had appeared somewhere in the maelstrom, and took off.

"Oh, Roxy," Mom wailed.

"Where's Niki?" I asked, searching the crowd for my younger sister.

Mom waved her hand. "I sent her over to a friend's house so she wouldn't have to see all this."

"And what's *this* Mom? What exactly did Dad do?"

She hung her head. "Looks like he stole money from the company, and when that wasn't enough, used our house and belongings as collateral."

Smacking me in the face with a baseball bat at the moment would not have had the effect my mom's news did on me.

Dad *stole*?

Then used our stuff as *collateral*?

Who was this man?

"And… and," she sniffed, "the worst is yet to come."

The *worst*? As if this wasn't bad enough?

"Dad hadn't made a payment on the house in months—"

And… that was why my tuition wasn't paid. Didn't need to be a college student to figure that shit out.

"Honey, you need to find a place to stay. Niki and your father and I are going to your aunt's house. I don't think there's room for you there."

Lovely. Just when I thought things couldn't get any worse.

In a burst of fury, I ran into the house to what was, or used to be, my room. The movers, or whatever they were called, hadn't gotten there yet. I grabbed a duffel from under my bed and stuffed a bunch of underwear, T-shirts, and jeans in it, then added some toiletries from the bathroom, just as one of the burly guys showed up in my doorway.

I froze.

But a kind expression washed over his face. "It's okay to take some personal items. Go ahead," he said, and left.

Huh. Nice of them.

After I stuffed my duffle full to bursting, I headed straight for my beat-up old car. I didn't know if that was on the list of things to 'seize,' but I wasn't taking any chances.

"Mom, I'll call you later," I hollered.

I hesitated to leave her but at that moment, what could I do to help? She stared as I pulled away, and when I was several blocks away, I figured I was safe from any further 'government seizure.' I pulled over and dialed Jessa.

"Roxy. How's it hanging, girl?" she asked in a happy, sing-song voice..

My voice broke. "Not so good."

Instant alarm changed her tone. "Oh shit. Where do you want to meet?"

"At the dorm?"

"On my way," she said.

4

ARROW MENKEN

"TABLE FOR ONE, PLEASE."

I smoothed down the front of my white shirt and followed the pretty hostess to a table by a window. I pulled a starched cloth napkin onto my lap, and smiled at the server filling up my water glass.

I didn't mind having lunch alone. In fact, I preferred it. Being in front of a classroom all day, and then surrounded by faculty in the department offices, was exhausting. Not that there was anything or anyone I didn't like. I just needed time to recharge every now and then.

And the faculty dining room was just the place.

It was quiet and distinguished, and reeked of everything I'd ever dreamed that would come with a life in academia.

There were some other things that came along with the success I'd enjoyed, which weren't so great. But the inconveniences were tolerable. It had been my life goal to become a professor and I was making it happen.

None of it was by accident.

I'd always dreamed of eating in places as nice as where I was now, and after years of hard work, it had become my reality.

"Hey Arrow, what are you doing here?"

My wish to have a solitary lunch flew out the window, but it was all good. My friend and housemate Baird helped himself to the second chair at my table, and once seated, rested his elbows on the starched white tablecloth.

"Hey, can you join me for lunch?" I offered as if it weren't a foregone conclusion.

"Sure, man. Love to. Don't have much time between student meetings and Boys Club stuff, but I am starving and am always happy to share a meal with my buddy."

If I couldn't have a lunch to myself, then the next best thing was to spend it with Baird. He was a good guy.

"So, things coming along with the Boys Club, then?" I asked.

He gestured excitedly. "Fucking awesome. The funding for the renovation of the old movie theater downtown is finalized. It's such an awesome space, totally derelict, but with massive potential. We've got the architectural plans and have chosen that big construction firm downtown. Everyone says they're the best. In fact they're breaking ground any day now"

He beamed. I knew his Boys Club work was important to him. Probably more important than even his work at the university. Baird and his big heart were all about helping people. I had massive respect for him.

I hadn't been by the theater in a while, not since Baird brought me there to share what, at the time, sounded like a crazy-ass renovation idea. It was full of bats and other nasty detritus, with large chunks of plaster falling off the walls and old wires hanging out of the ceiling. But he was leading the charge to clean it up and turn it into housing. It would become an investment asset for the Club, and provide transitional housing to families in need, as well.

"Congrats," I said. "The work you've done is really paying off."

He shook his head modestly. "It's the work of a bunch of people, including you. I mean, look at all the time you spent putting together our financials."

I was a finance professor, after all.

But it felt good to contribute to the cause. Really good. Especially since I wasn't so different from those kids the Boys Club served.

Not many people knew from looking at me in my expensively tailored clothes, and habit of fine dining, that I'd started out with next to nothing. I mean, my friends, including Baird, knew. But that was it. I didn't need anyone fawning over the 'success story' that I was. I got enough of that when I returned to my hometown.

Something I avoided at all costs. Too many memories. Too many regrets.

"Well, look at that," Baird said, squinting across the dining room while adjusting his wire-framed glasses. "Interesting."

I followed his gaze but saw nothing besides other faculty and the black-outfitted servers waiting on them. I turned back to my salmon filet. I'd never even tasted salmon until I'd graduated college and was living in New York, working on Wall Street. What a fucking new world all that had been.

When Baird continued staring, I got curious, and craned my neck to follow his gaze. What the hell was he up to?

"What is it?" I asked.

He gestured with his chin. "See that server? The one with the long blonde ponytail?"

I slipped my own glasses on. "Yeah. I think she might be in one of my classes. You know her?"

The longer I looked, the more certain I was that I'd seen her around. She was willowy and graceful with her all-black waiter garb and blonde hair pulled into a tidy ponytail. She wasn't the kind of woman a man forgot.

Which, I supposed, was why Baird couldn't keep his eyes off her.

He finally focused on his lunch and dove into his bacon cheeseburger. "She's one of my advisees. Roxy Vandenberg. When I was at my Boys Club meeting yesterday, at the hotel downtown, I saw her from a distance. She's a maid there. And now she's working here. Christ, how many jobs does this girl have?" he said, turning back to watch her.

Damn. I'd seen that look before. You don't work around young women in their prime and not notice the abundance of charms their youth and beauty offered. But when a man couldn't take his eyes off a student, well that was another story all together.

It was understandable. Completely.

And also potentially dangerous.

"Hey, you don't happen to be thinking with your little head over there, are ya?"

We'd all been there.

His attention snapped back to me, and he rubbed his hand over his face. "Maybe. I can't lie. But I met with her just yesterday. She's having financial problems and apparently now juggling a couple jobs. Gotta hand it to her. That's not an easy road, going to school full-time and trying to pay your way."

I wasn't surprised when Baird jumped to his feet and waved until he caught her attention. She squinted for a moment, then headed our way with a water pitcher in hand.

"Mr. Priestly, Professor Menken, nice to see you. I hope you're enjoying your lunch," she said politely.

She smiled, revealing a gap between her teeth. The slight imperfection somehow made her even more beautiful. My best friend from high school had one just like it. Probably still did, for all I knew. I don't think orthodontia was ever in the cards for him.

I could see why Baird was smitten.

I couldn't lie. I was a bit, too.

"Hey, Roxy, call me Baird." He looked over at me. "And sounds like you know this guy here, too," he said, pointing at me.

She nodded and fixed her gaze on me, holding me hostage. Seriously. For a moment I couldn't move. Or speak.

How did she do that? Did she even *know* she was doing that?

"Yes, I do. Hello, Professor. How was your salmon?"

I recovered my senses, and waved away her formality. "You can call me Arrow. As much as I love being a professor, being *called* one still kind of freaks me out."

She gave a small laugh.

I wished she had time to sit and join us for our after-lunch coffee. But the way she was looking back over her shoulder told me she was a conscientious employee. She had tables to wait on, and hopefully money to make. College wasn't cheap, and not everyone got a scholarship like I'd been lucky enough to. Yup, I'd gotten a one-way ticket out of town, something I was still conflicted over, at least when I let myself think about it long enough. Which I seldom did.

"Roxy, how many jobs do you have?" Baird asked. "I saw you from a distance at the hotel yesterday, and here you are, now."

A pink tinge washed over her face, and my heart broke for her a little. I knew what it was like to be ashamed.

"Oh, you were at the hotel?" she asked stiffly. "Yes, I

work there as you know, and just picked up this shift in the restaurant today from another server who couldn't make it in. It's just a one-day thing. Found it on the job board. Right now I'm pretty much taking anything I can get."

Resignation replaced her flush.

Baird nodded at her. "So… things looking up any? You know, regarding what we talked about?"

She glanced at me, clearly wondering whether Baird had told me of her situation. So I decided to clear the air.

"Roxy, Baird tells me you are having some financial problems. There's nothing wrong with that. Happens to college students all the time."

He chuckled. "Shit, happens to people out of college all the time, too."

She smiled with appreciation. "Yes, well, it just caught me by surprise, that's all," she said. "And to be honest, things, if you can believe it, are actually worse than I'd thought."

Her voice cracked on that last word, but she swallowed hard and shook it off.

Christ, did I have a lot in common with this girl.

Baird frowned. "How so? Any new developments?"

She sighed and spoke matter-of-factly. "My parents' house has been foreclosed on, and some government agency came and seized most of their belongings. My dad… did something illegal, I'm told. I have no details, though. Not yet, anyway."

Holy cow. This woman was carrying the weight of the world on her shoulders.

And just like Baird always said about his charity work, he couldn't help *everyone*, but he could help *someone*. Was this my opportunity to do the same?

"I… I'm wondering if I can help in any way, Roxy," I said.

She pressed her lips together. "Oh. No, that's okay. I mean, thank you." She looked over her shoulder again.

Baird tapped the table with his fingers like he did when he was thinking. "Roxy, you came to me for help. This is not the time for pride. This is the time you grab at every opportunity that comes your way, no matter how small or insignificant. I don't mean to lecture, but you're a determined woman. Look at you busting your ass with any job you can find. Let us help."

She looked relieved and nodded. "You're right, I guess. I'm just not sure what else to do."

"I've got one idea for you," I said, "come to my personal finance class and discuss your circumstances. You can be our case study."

Her eyes flew open. "No way! Tell a classroom of people about my pathetic situation?"

I shook my head. "You can't look at it that way. Besides, the gig pays one hundred dollars. I know that won't cover your tuition, but it's probably a hell of a lot easier money than hours of serving club sandwiches to stuffy college professors."

That got her laughing. "You have a point. I didn't even know there *was* a personal finance class."

"You have to understand personal finance before you can learn corporate finance, don't you think?" I asked.

It was shocking how many business majors had no interest in learning how to manage their own money. Proceed at your own risk, I always said.

"You might take this class eventually too, you know," I added. "It's an elective but I highly recommend it. Over almost any other elective in the business management school."

"Well then, I guess I'm sold," she said.

If her father had financial troubles, then she definitely could stand to learn to do things differently than her parents. Break the generational pattern, like I had.

"The class may even come up with solutions to your problem. Give it a chance," I said.

Baird was beaming. "You never know where support will come from. Let's talk later. You gotta get back to work."

She giggled. "Yes, I do. Talk to you both later. And, thank you."

Baird took a long draw on his coffee. "And *that* is why I love the work I do. I have to deal with the occasional bone-headed student who couldn't give a shit about college, but I mostly get to help folks like Roxy who just need a little push to see their way forward."

"You're good at what you do, Baird," I said. "Hey, why isn't she applying for scholarships?"

He sighed. "It's late for this semester, and her grades

are somewhat mediocre, probably because of all the hours she works."

It was a vicious cycle. You work to have the money for school, but the work takes away from study time.

I was pretty sure I'd come from beginnings far more humble than anything Roxy had ever seen. There was one scholarship offered by my small town to our high school. I'd competed against another kid for it, and won. I got my college education, and he did not. The way things had played out haunted me from time to time, and seeing Roxy's situation brought it all back.

I had a life no one else in my town ever had. Especially the guy who'd once called me his best friend.

5

ROXY VANDENBERG

"Damn, Roxy. That's some messed up shit."

Gee, thanks.

But Jessa was right. I was in the middle of some very messed up shit.

"Rox, what do you think your dad did to bring this on?" Birdie asked.

It was a good question and one I wanted an answer to, myself. Not that it would change anything.

It wouldn't get my tuition magically paid. It wouldn't put my parents' things back in their house.

The house they no longer owned.

I filled my cheeks with air and blew it out slowly, trying to release some of the tightness in my chest. It didn't help. "I have no idea, Birdie, but it must have been pretty bad. I've called him and he won't answer, and when I called his work, they said he was no longer employed there. The whole situation is majorly fucked."

Jessa let out a long, low whistle. "He must have stolen money from his employer or something."

Birdie nudged her. "Jessa, don't be so dramatic. Roxy doesn't need that right now."

She frowned. "Why? What the hell else could it be? And if their house and property were being seized, he's in trouble with not only his employer but the government, too."

As much as it made me sick to hear it, I had a feeling she was probably right.

"Let's focus on the positive," Birdie said, laying a gentle hand on my arm. "We need solutions right now, the first one being helping Roxy with a place to live. Sweetie, you stay here in the dorm for as long as you need. Jessa and I will be in and out since we spend most of the time over at the guys' houses. No one will bother you, not even the sex queen next door."

"Is she back this semester?" I asked.

Birdie and Jessa looked at each other.

"From the noise I heard the other day, it would seem so," Jessa said.

Hey, who were they to judge? They each had their own regular sex fests to enjoy, thanks to the hot professors who'd fallen for them.

I was happy for them. I really was. But I didn't think their type of arrangement would work for me. I mean, I had a couple hot professors, for sure, like Arrow Menken. And then there was my academic advisor, Baird, whom I'd thrown myself at when I was bawling like a baby. But I was otherwise so tongue-tied around these gorgeous men they probably thought I was a total idiot.

And now that these two also knew of my financial problems, they'd be avoiding me like I had leprosy, no doubt. Not that I thought they'd want to hang out with me otherwise. Really.

"You guys are some lifesaving bitches," I said, unsuccessfully hiding the hitch in my voice.

"You'd do the same for us," Jessa said, rubbing my back.

She was right.

"So what did the advisor say?" Birdie asked.

"Well, he said he'd check out some resources for me. But my finance professor, who I ran into when I was working in the faculty dining room, made me an interesting offer when he learned about my situation. I'll probably say no, but it was nice of him to try to help."

Birdie and Jessa both looked at me, waiting.

"Well, what was the offer?" Jessa asked with a smile.

I knew that look.

"Nothing like that. Geez, you guys."

Not that I would mind a little nook-nook with the man. I mean, his piercing blue eyes and shy smile probably brought a lot of female students to their knees. Some guys, too, probably. But that was so far off the table for me that I didn't even let myself think about it. Except for late at night when I was in bed alone. Luckily, I'd stuffed my purple vibe in my duffle bag when I bailed on my parents' place, and my little electronic boyfriend had served me well the past few nights when

I had a lot of shit on my mind and had the dorm room to myself.

A little self-love was often just what the doctor ordered. So to speak.

"So, my finance professor, Arrow Menken teaches a personal finance class where he has guest speakers come in. He said if I came by the class and shared my… problem, I'd get paid one hundred dollars."

Jessa whooped. "That sounds like the easiest money I've ever heard of."

But I shook my head. "No way. I don't want to share my shitshow with a classroom of strangers. Are you kidding? Talk about humiliating."

"You could always model nude for art classes like I do," Jessa offered.

"Are you still doing that?" I asked. I'd thought all that was behind her, thanks to the new men in her life who were taking care of things. All sorts of things…

Jessa shrugged. "I like it. Plus, it's hot as fuck. I'll model for one of Indy's classes and it gets us so worked up, casting glances at each other throughout class, that the moment everyone's gone I'm on my knees sucking his—"

I held my hand up like a stop sign.

Birdie laughed. "Don't talk to me about humiliation. It was you guys who got me to write that freaking paper about being a virgin that was read by two English professors and a TA."

Was she still griping about that?

"And look how that turned out for you, Birdie. You should be fucking thanking us." I laughed.

Jessa, always the optimist, turned the conversation back to the personal finance class. "Roxy, what if someone in the class has a good solution? What if someone knows of a last-minute scholarship or a job that pays better than the hotel?"

I scoffed. I didn't mean to be rude. It was just that I'd been let down so much over the last few days that I had little or no faith in humanity. "What are the chances of that, of some student solving all my problems?"

Birdie threw her hands up. "Look. One hundred bucks is not going to solve anything but for the amount of time it will take to earn it, I say go for it. Cripes, sign *me* up," she laughed.

Yeah right. She pretty much had it made. But she also had a point. It was always nice to earn an extra hundred bucks.

"I'll think about it. But in the meantime, I'm starving. Anyone down for a delicious dining hall meal?"

"Good job. I'd call that a success."

I wasn't so sure. I watched the last of Professor Menken's class filter out the door into the hallway, happily chatting, as the last shreds of what little pride I had left followed them, leaving me with a big, fat void where my self-respect used to live.

It hadn't just been embarrassing to get up in front of these people, it was all I could do not to run from the room and hide for the rest of my life.

Why had I agreed to bare my soul to a classroom of fellow students who looked at me like I had two heads? My challenges were so far out of the realm of anything they knew, unloading on them was pretty much a waste of their time and mine.

Not so much for the professor, though.

Did he know something I didn't?

It had started off painlessly enough. I just explained to the class that I didn't have the money for this semester's tuition.

"Get a job."

"Come back next semester."

"Put it on a credit card."

"Ask your parents."

Really? How did these people get into college to begin with? And the conversation only got more stupid from there when I foolishly volunteered that the major part of the problem was it was looking like my dad might be some sort of criminal or something.

The class shifted from personal finance to a sort of Perry Mason episode.

"Are you gonna turn him in?"

"Hey, I know a good lawyer."

"You know, you might be culpable, too. I'd leave town if I were you."

That's when the fifty-minute class ended. Without a word from the professor, everyone slammed their books closed and stampeded for the door. I continued to stand at the front of the class like I had for an agonizing fifty minutes, watching them funnel out like the place was on fire.

I pinched myself to make sure I was still alive. Because I sure didn't want to be.

"Well, um, thank you, Professor Menken," I said, avoiding his gaze while I gathered my things.

I really wanted to club him in the knees, but while I might come from a family of supposed criminals, they *had* taught me manners.

He propped his butt on the edge of the desk in the front of the room. The one I'd tried to hide behind all class.

"First off," he said, "call me Arrow. Really. And like I said before, Roxy, there is no shame in your situation. I know. Because I've been there."

Um, yeah right. Professor Menken—Arrow—was the epitome of money with his expensive shoes, starched, monogrammed shirts, and thick silk ties. The man had a freaking PhD, and rumor had it he'd worked on Wall Street before becoming an academic. He was loaded as fuck.

I found it hard to believe he'd ever scraped for anything in his life. Or had a lawbreaker for a father, for that matter.

"You're doubting me," he said.

Busted. Was he a mind-reader, too?

And he really had to stop looking at me with those goddamn blue eyes.

"Oh, well, um, you don't seem… I mean, look at you. You're nothing like me."

My voice petered out. I was not in the business of diving into the personal lives of my professors, even if they had invited me to use their first names.

He hoisted himself onto the desk and crossed his arms. It was clear he expected me to stay and listen to him.

Yeah right. His sob story. He was probably going to belly ache about how he got a used car for his sixteenth birthday rather than a new one like all the other kids in his high school. I knew his type. I was surrounded by them all day long.

But I nodded attentively, doing my best to hide that I thought he was full of shit.

"Roxy, I got the *one* scholarship available to kids in my high school. The *only* one. I competed for that, and my getting it changed the trajectory of my life. If I hadn't, I'd be back in the small town where I'd grown up, eking out a living just like my parents had. There'd be none of this," he said, gesturing at his clothes, and then the university we were surrounded by.

"I was goddamn lucky," he continued. "But I also busted my ass. When I landed my job on Wall Street, I was the biggest hick anyone in the firm had ever seen. To this day, I still think they hired me because they felt sorry for me. They had to teach me how to dress, how to dine in nice restaurants. All that shit. And yes, it was embarrassing. But I lived through it, did a good job, and became respected by everyone I worked with."

No way. Not him.

Absolutely not.

But would he really be lying about something like that?

I tried to keep my expression neutral. I really did.

But he saw right through me. "I know I don't look like I come from humble beginnings. But I do. After being a trader for some years, I went back to school for my PhD and became an academic. I support my parents and one disabled sister. Contrary to what you might think, I am *not* the walking poster child for privilege."

I swallowed hard, feeling kind of shitty. You just never knew about people.

"That's… incredible. I had no idea," I said, staring at my feet. "I'm the first in my family to go to college, too. It's my dream. I want it more than anything."

He shrugged. "I get that Roxy. And hey, I don't tell a lot of people my story. It's none of their business. But I feel like for you to trust me, you need to know who I am. Now, how about I walk you to your car? It's dark out already."

For an instant, I didn't want him to see the old piece of crap I drove, which I'd bought for one thousand dollars my senior year of high school, and which for some lucky reason, kept running with a minimum of repairs.

But then I figured, shit. The man knew my story and now I knew his. There were no surprises left.

Or so I thought.

I put the key in my car door lock and pulled open the door. "Thank you so much, Professor Menk—I mean, Arrow."

It felt kind of cool to use his first name. Not at all weird.

Even under the dim street lamp, his piercing blue eyes glittered as he smiled. "My pleasure," he said.

Shit. Did I hear a little growl at the end of that?

No way. Imagining things.

Calm down, girl.

I plunked into my driver seat, leaving the door open to keep him around for a few more seconds, but when I turned the key, the engine remained silent.

I looked up at him and laughed. "This happens all the time. You know how these jalopies are."

He leaned closer to get a look at my dashboard, and damn if he didn't smell nice.

I turned the key again.

And again, no sound.

Fuck, fuck, fuckity, fuck.

"Let me give it a sec," I said. "You don't have to wait. I don't want to hold you up, Arrow."

I'd said his name again, and damn if it didn't feel like a warm Hershey's Kiss in my mouth. Melty and delicious. Would it be weird if I said it about ten more times?

But I needed to focus, and my car wasn't starting.

"Guess I'm stuck," I said, smiling weakly.

I didn't have far to go, just to the other side of campus to get to Jessa and Birdie's dorm room, but I couldn't leave my car where it was overnight.

Why, universe? Haven't you shit on me quite enough, lately?

I got out of the car and slammed the door, but when I looked over at Arrow, he was calmly talking on his cell phone.

He slipped it back into his pocket. "Okay. Your car is being towed to my mechanic. Let's go."

Um, what?

But I was so speechless that he would take charge that way, I just followed him.

He settled me into the front seat of a late-model Mercedes, and started to drive. I didn't even know where we were going. I couldn't bring myself to ask. I was part total fucking loser, part so excited to be in this man's car, the fluttering in my chest made it near impossible to speak.

"Roxy, could you put your seatbelt on, please?"

"Yes. Yes of course," I mumbled, and obediently complied.

How was it that my professor, who had just hooked me up with one hundred dollars, who was having my car towed to a repair shop, and who was driving me somewhere—where, I did not know— was now telling me to put my seatbelt on?

How fucking weird was life?

He drove out of the campus onto the city streets,

following a route I knew from my high school joyriding days, toward one of the nicer neighborhoods in town, one with wide sidewalks, sprawling front yards, and mature oaks that draped over the streets like an archway into a different universe.

Professor Menken might have started out in my world, but he sure as hell didn't live there anymore.

"I'm guessing we're going to your house?" I asked, my fingers itching on the door handle as I tried to remember which pocket of my backpack held my pepper spray.

He nodded while he pulled into the garage and the door closed behind us.

I knew my alarm radar should have been screaming that this was not right. Stranger danger! Get away now! Save yourself!

Was I fucking crazy?

Maybe. Probably. Most definitely.

But I didn't care.

Just, for a moment, I wanted someone else to make decisions for me. I could usually handle my own shit, but just once, I wanted someone to tell me what I needed to do. To show me the way. 'Cause I sure as hell couldn't figure it out on my own.

I had to admit, I was scared. And being scared was exhausting. I didn't know where my messed-up life was taking me, but I wanted someone else to take the wheel, if only temporarily.

And Arrow was just the person to do that.

I trusted him. He knew my challenges. He knew my triumphs and failures.

He'd lived through his own.

And now look at him. Successful. Elegant. Smart. Kind.

I'll have some of that, thank you.

I followed him into a house decorated with dark, masculine tones, the walls covered in large, abstract paintings, one of which particularly caught my eye.

I couldn't be sure, but was it a woman on her knees in front of a man? I didn't have time to study it though, hustling to keep up with him as he directed me straight to a guest room.

He flicked on a light. "Here you go. There are towels and other things in your bathroom. Holler if you need anything. Oh, and help yourself to anything in the kitchen."

Before I could say anything—even thank you—he headed into the room next door to mine, and closed his door with a soft *click*.

My head was reeling with the strangeness of what had just occurred. What the hell was I doing in the guest room of the home of one of my professors? Why hadn't I just asked him to take me to the dorm where I'd been crashing?

Had I wanted this and somehow conveyed it to him? Maybe I had… and maybe I wanted even more.

I pressed the lock on my door because of course, and started to text Jessa and Birdie. But I stopped. I knew they had new lives with their professors, but I didn't want them to assume I was doing the same. I wasn't hooking up with a professor. Ever. It just wasn't my thing.

No matter how piercing their blue eyes were. Or how good they smelled.

But there I was. So I did the only thing I could think of—I got ready for bed starting by brushing my teeth with the new toothbrush and paste I'd found in one of the vanity drawers.

As I crawled under my bed's fluffy white down comforter, there was a noise coming from the next room over.

The room Professor Menken had gone to.

Arrow's room.

And it was a lot like the noises I heard in Jessa and Birdie's dorm on a fairly regular basis, coming from the other rooms around me.

The heavy breathing and slight slapping of skin left no doubt. Surefire signs of a man jerking off.

Holy shit. Was Arrow, my professor, rubbing one out in the room right next door to mine?

I pictured him with his proper clothes tossed onto the floor in a pile, climbing on top of his sprawling king sized bed. He fell back into the pillows and comforter, butt naked, with his erection pointing angrily toward the ceiling.

After getting comfortable, he spread his legs and spit on his open palm. Gripping his cock, he started by lightly fisting himself, grunting at the initial sensation. With his free hand, he crammed a pillow behind his head, propping himself up so he could watch himself.

After reaching the root of his dick, his hand traveled back up and opened slightly when he ran his palm over his cockhead, gathering a drop or two of precum. He closed his fist around the head again and squeezed tighter, until he almost winced.

While I pictured him, my own hand slipped beneath my covers, where I found my folds wet and excited thanks to my healthy imagination.

Imagination? To hell with that. I was listening to the real thing. There was nothing imagined about it. My finance professor was in the next room, stroking his dick.

The question was, was he thinking about me? Because I sure as hell was thinking about him.

Was he imagining my walking into the room, dropping whatever I was wearing, and joining him on the bed, where I opened my legs to show how he'd excited me? Was he thinking about watching me slide a finger inside myself, then pulling it out and to my mouth for a taste? Was he thinking about my straddling him, reverse cowgirl style, so he could watch my pussy swallow him whole while he rubbed his thumb against my asshole with one hand and held a fistful of my long hair in his other?

Because I sure as fuck was thinking about that, myself.

My fingers rubbed my clit faster, while through the wall, Arrow's breathing grew raspier. Within moments, my own climax built to the point where I was shudder-ing. Every part of my body, save for my working hand, tensed, waiting for the explosion I knew was going to rock me.

I pictured him speeding his strokes until his hand moved so fast it was a blur, and when streams of thick, white cum spurted from his dick, his voice jolted me out of my fantasy and back to reality.

Pushing me to my edge, of course.

I held my breath to hear him, guttural and unfamil-iar, so unlike the proper finance professor I was used to listening to at the front of the classroom.

His language was coarse and lewd. And I fucking loved it. "Take my cock, Roxy. Fucking take it," he grunted.

He *had* been thinking of me. Just like I'd been thinking of him.

I did my best to stay quiet, but I exploded anyway with a great moan, turned over, and fell fast asleep, wondering how I would ever focus in his class again.

6

SILAS FOX

Fuck if I didn't hate Mondays.

Oh. Wait.

It wasn't Monday. It was Tuesday.

Fortunately, I had only one architecture class to teach on Tuesdays and Thursdays, and while it was a long one, nearly three hours, it didn't begin until afternoon. So I spent my mornings on those days grading stuff, emailing students, and working on my own, personal projects like the house I was having built, among other things.

I often let myself sleep in then, too.

In the ratty old sweats I slept in when it was cold outside, I padded over to the thousand-dollar espresso machine Arrow had insisted he needed in his all-stainless designer kitchen, and poured myself, admittedly, some of the best Italian coffee I'd ever had.

I couldn't deny it. The goddamn machine was incredible. As was the coffee it made. I'd miss it when I moved into my own house, currently under construction. Fuck it. Maybe I'd even get one when all was said and done. I'd still need my morning coffee.

While my new place was by far the biggest project I had underway, I was also helping my buddy Baird with his Boys Club renovation of an old movie theater. Through nothing less than blood, sweat, and tears, the man had managed to raise funds for the project, the likes of which the town had never seen. So, I took advantage of having the house to myself, and returned to my big laptop, set up on the kitchen table, and picked over the designs I'd been working on for him.

But something was missing. I mean, not really missing. Everything that needed to be in the architectural drawings was there. Hell, we'd been granted the permits we needed by the city, so I knew I'd done a solid job. Even so, I continued to tweak things. The stairs connecting the second floor of the old theater to what would be the new, third floor, seemed... awkward.

And I didn't like awkward. No architect did, really, but I particularly detested it. The bane of my existence. I needed my designs to flow. I demanded it of them, actually.

I could be obsessive that way.

While I stared at my CAD program, a door softly opened and closed on the other side of the house. I'd been waiting for that sound.

It had been a good time, living the bachelor life with Arrow and Baird. They'd both gotten me involved in their charity work with the Boys Club, and my skills turned out to be a perfect fit. We made a great team on the old movie theater renovation. Baird was spearheading it all while Arrow dealt with the finances, and I delivered the vision of turning the derelict old building into housing for families in need.

It felt good to focus on something other than teaching, and my life at the university. And it felt really good to be designing something that wasn't just theoretical, and that would help the community. I was honestly excited to see it actually, eventually, come to life and be inhabited by real human beings who deserved a decent place to live.

I hadn't felt that way in a long time.

But my attention was redirected to another noise coming from the far reaches of the house.

Arrow and Baird had left hours ago, to get their workouts in at the campus athletic center before their day with students began, so I knew whatever I was hearing was not from them.

But there was no cause for alarm. I'd heard a... guest in the house the night before, and figured this person was just starting their day.

I had half a mind to see who it was and what they were up to, but it was my policy to mind my own business in matters of roommate life. I hadn't lived with other people in years, and I'd promised myself when Arrow had invited me to bunk up with him, that I'd keep my head down and stay out of the other guys' lives so long as they stayed out of mine.

They were my friends, and I didn't want our short time living together to throw any kinks in our relationship.

So if someone had a 'friend' over the night before, it was none of my damn business. But that didn't stop me from being curious.

Especially since I'd heard our house guest, whose room shared a wall with mine, having a little fun in her room the night before. All by herself.

How'd I know she was alone? I'd heard Arrow show her to the room and abruptly say goodnight. I wasn't sure why he invited a woman home only to show her to the guest room, but the man must have had his reasons.

And the hot little noises she made as she pleasured herself were a thoroughly unexpected delight. I'd have to thank him later for setting her up right next to me. It was downright awesome of him.

I'd been up reading, so I heard her wash up and get ready for bed. And when her bed began to rock just the slightest bit, it was without a doubt clear what she was up to. When her breathing got heavy and raspy, I took my own good time in hand.

Literally.

It was beyond hot, listening to a woman moan and sigh, with no idea what she looked like. Not that I had any shortage of beautiful women in my imagination to jerk off to, but a situation like this let the mind go wild.

Was she curvy or slim?

Dark skinned or light?

Blue eyes or brown?

Long hair or short?

Big tits or small?

Not that it really mattered. Her little gasps and sighs, which led to a growing, then final, moan when she achieved her climax, set off my own as I collected my streams of ejaculate in the extra towel I kept in my nightstand for just that purpose.

Fucking hot, jerking off to the sounds of a stranger.

A stranger who was still in my house. Well, Arrow's house.

"Good morning," a woman's voice tentatively said.

Holy fuck. I nearly went through the roof at the sound of her so close behind me. While I'd known someone was in the house, I hadn't heard her coming and had no idea she was headed in my direction. I'd assumed she'd dress and slip out the side door without a word.

But I was glad she hadn't because when I whipped around, I saw she was a pleasure to behold. Well done, Arrow. Well done.

Our houseguest was a tall, thin blonde with terribly adorable bedhead, bundled up in one of Arrow's terrycloth bathrobes.

How did I know it was Arrow's? Because his initials were on it, like they were on nearly all his shit.

Monograms were his thing.

I jumped to my feet. "Oh. Hello. I'm Silas."

I extended my hand because I didn't know what

else to do. I mean, I wasn't going to say, *hey I heard you jerking off last night and found it quite enjoyable.*

Yeah, no.

"Hello. I'm Roxy. Roxy Vandenberg."

She returned a healthy, firm handshake. Hopefully with the same hand she'd pleasured herself the night before. I was tempted to sniff it.

"I didn't know anyone lived here with Arrow."

Apparently not.

She looked around the kitchen, her gaze settling on our fancy espresso machine when I realized she was actually avoiding looking at *me.*

I looked down at myself in ratty sweats that were probably a little too clingy to be seen in mixed company. And I had no shirt on at all.

I hiked them up so they at least covered the top of my pubes, and reached for a jacket someone had left on the back of a kitchen chair.

As I started to pull it on, I thought fuck it. She'd already seen my pierced nipple, bicep tattoos, and whatever else my immodest clothing was revealing. I mean, shit, she was wearing another man's bathrobe.

We were kind of even, if you asked me.

"I'm an architecture professor at the university. Camping out here until my own house is finished. Are you a student?"

She nodded, still avoiding looking at me, setting her gaze on my open laptop and plans for the movie theater.

"I'm a business major. My car broke down so

Professor Menk—I mean, Arrow—gave me a lift here. I slept in the guest room."

Thank god for little miracles.

"Whatcha working on?" she asked.

For a moment, I didn't know what she was talking about. All I could do was stare at her mop of bedhead and think that the gap between her teeth was about the most fucking sexy thing I'd ever seen in my life.

Truly.

It was in sharp contrast to her otherwise sultry presence, adding a *fuck you* that was unexpected. And delicious.

How many people these days ran around with gaps in their teeth when we were surrounded by dental work that delivered perfectly straight, overly whitened teeth? Not a hell of a lot.

She was… real.

But I'd forgotten my manners. "Coffee?" I asked.

She bounced up and down a little in her bare feet, unbothered by my near-nakedness.

I was in love.

"Please, yes. I would love some."

As soon as I'd handed her a big, steaming mug, because—I couldn't deny it—I wanted her to stick around as long as possible, I pulled a chair around the table so she could sit next to me. *Right* next to me.

"Back to your question about what I'm working on. You know the old, closed movie theater downtown?" I asked.

Her eyes widened. "Yeah. I used to go there as a kid. I was so sad when they shut it down."

Then she was going to be thrilled with this project.

"The local Boys Club chapter raised the funds to purchase it, and I'm working on the design to turn it into residences."

A wobbly smile spread across her face. "No way. That's… great."

Something about the way she said it indicated otherwise.

But I was sure it was just the awkwardness of our meeting.

So, I nodded at my computer. "I'm working on the architectural designs right here."

"Oh. Can I look?" she asked.

I took her on a tour of the 3-d design. "We expect to get ten units out of the space when all is said and done. Four on the second floor with six on the third, and offices at the street level."

"Wow. So you'll be adding a third floor?" she asked, leaning closer to the computer and giving me a peek inside her robe at her firm little tits. "That's a big project."

I squirmed in my chair and pressed an arm into my lap. It wouldn't do to get a hard-on just then.

She sat back in her chair, sipping her coffee, but looking like she was dying to bolt. "It's going to be… so nice. Look… at all the work you've done. Which… which firm is building it for you?" she asked in a shaky voice.

Jesus, she was tense. Much as I wanted to continue chatting with her, she probably needed to be on her way.

"The same firm that built the new athletic center for the university. They're the best, and their bid was the strongest."

She continued staring at my screen.

"Looks like you see the same problem I do with the plans. See here, this is the thing bugging me. I just don't like these stairs. I can't put my finger on it but they… don't work."

She leaned toward the computer again, taking in the entire visual. "Why don't you move them… here?" she said, pointing to just a few feet from where I currently had them.

I shrugged. It wasn't a bad idea. The beauty of CAD was that you could mess around and try pretty much anything. That didn't mean I wanted to end up with an Escher drawing of staircases leading nowhere, but I could humor the girl and give her suggestion a try.

So I rearranged the stairs, studying the new configuration.

And you know what? It was fucking awesome.

"I'll be damned," I said. "This works. It really works."

She clapped her hands together with satisfaction.

"Are you sure you don't want to study architecture?" I asked. "It sounds like you have some experience in this area."

She waved off my suggestion. "No way. Architects have to work too hard."

She had that right. At least for the ones who worked in firms. That's why I was at Wellshire. Academic life wasn't easy, but it also wasn't miserable.

"So how did you know to—" I started to ask.

But she interrupted me by jumping to her feet. "Oh, um, my father… well, he's a contractor, or rather a subcontractor. Or, he used to be. But hey, I gotta head out. Nice meeting you, Silas."

I watched her speed walk away, her ass shaking under her borrowed terry cloth robe, when I glanced at the time on my computer.

Shit. I needed to get ready to leave, too.

Rushing past the guest room where she'd spent the night, I noticed she'd left her door open a few inches. The shower was running, so I started to pull her door closed when I heard her yell.

"Shit! There's no shampoo."

I couldn't help but laugh when I closed the door, but then had an idea.

I returned to the guest room with shampoo from my own bathroom and slowly opened the door. The water was still running in the bathroom, so I shouted over the noise.

"Hey, Roxy! Did you say you need shampoo?"

"Yeah. Do you have any?" she called back.

I certainly did.

I crossed the room, but remained outside the bathroom. "Here. I'll stand behind the door," I said, stretching my arm inside, extending the bottle.

The glass shower door slipped open. "Damn. I can't quite reach it. Hold on."

Wet feet slapped the bathroom floor's tile, and from the other side of the door, Roxy took the shampoo. But just as I was withdrawing my arm, she shrieked, and grabbed the door as she lost her footing.

Yeah, those tiles were slippery under wet feet. Arrow had insisted on them even though I told him they were an impractical design choice.

In Roxy's momentary panic, her grabbing the door for balance had yanked it wide open. While I tried to look away, I was able to catch her arm and keep her from completely wiping out on the bathroom floor.

After slipping and sliding, she had her feet back under her, and I pulled the door closed and returned to my own room.

But not before getting a good look at her. Naked. Dripping wet. Glistening like a beautiful water nymph with bouncy little tits and a shaved pussy.

Yeah, I fucking looked at the whole thing.

I hustled back to my own shower, where I had some important business of my own to take care of.

7

ROXY VANDENBERG

"Bet you thought you were really slick this morning, sneaking out of Professor Menken's house. My sorority is on the same street."

I looked up to see my class's, and possibly the entire university's, resident mean girl.

Paloma Saardi.

Of course someone with a name like that would be a nasty bitch.

She'd never paid any attention to me. Until now. I wasn't usually on the radar of the genetically and socially gifted universe that revolved around people like Paloma. I was more of a nameless moon, reluctantly orbiting with no option to either get closer or further away.

And that's exactly how I preferred it.

I had my posse of friends and didn't need any more. Especially people like Paloma.

I'd snagged a second-row seat in my business

analytics class, which I was currently only auditing, thanks to my tuition payment issue. I preferred the second row in the cavernous auditorium classroom, given the choice. The first row was too eager, but the second was close enough that the teacher could easily see me, which meant I had to pay attention.

No dozing off that close to the front. It was the perfect compromise.

But because so many other students had the same idea, I always got there early. I could be vicious when it came to my seat.

So while I was waiting for class to kick off, I'd gone onto the university's app, where I'd clicked on the 'faculty' tab. I needed to know who the hell Silas the architecture professor was, aside from being a very good-looking man doing charity work who'd also, incidentally, seen me naked and dripping wet.

After I'd used his shampoo, I dried as quickly as I could, pulled my clothes on, and tiptoed out the side door without saying goodbye. I figured he'd seen enough of me for one day.

But that didn't mean I didn't find him dreamy.

I was initially mortified to have slid on that damn tile floor, but when I watched his eyes do a quick once-over—that's all there really was time for—something inside me got all warm and gooey. Of course, he quickly pulled the bathroom door shut to save me from further humiliation, but things had been set in motion.

I jumped back in the shower, finished cleaning myself, and reached to turn the water off.

But I stopped.

I watched the warm water sluice down the front of my body, over and around my breasts, to the V between my legs, where it momentarily collected before running down my inner thighs.

Silas would have enjoyed the view also, as I supposed Arrow would have, given the noises he'd made the night before.

I imagined Silas delivering his bottle of shampoo in a slightly different way.

First, he'd knock.

"Yes?" I'd holler.

"Here's the shampoo you needed."

The bathroom door made a small *click* as it opened and I turned to watch him enter the room. He was blurry though the steamed-up glass shower wall, but I could still see the passion that had washed over his face when he got his 'accidental' look at me.

He held the shampoo bottle just out of my reach. Of course.

"Roxy, have you ever had your hair washed? In the shower? By a man?"

What? Did he really just say something about washing hair?

Washing *my* hair?

"Um, no, not really, I mean it sounds fun, but I'm not sure—"

Before I could stop babbling, the shower door opened and a naked Silas joined me.

The steamy water instantly bounced off his body,

first soaking his hair and his beautiful face, then running down his arms over his tattoos, to his hard pecs with a pierced nipple, finally reaching the thin line of hair leading to his...

Oh. My. God.

He was hard.

And he was huge.

Holyshitsholyshitholyshit.

I stepped a few inches to the side so he could douse himself entirely in the shower stream. But instead of warming himself up, he turned me to face away, gathering my hair into one long single, thick rope. Seconds later, he was massaging the most delicious smelling shampoo into my hair, alternatively rubbing my scalp with the pads of his fingers, and snaking the lather all the way to my ends. I braced myself with flat palms on the shower wall in front of me, hoping my shaking knees would continue to keep me upright.

He moved closer, his lips touching my ear. "How do you like it, Roxy?"

I let my head drop back. "Amazing," I breathed.

It was all I could say, really.

His erection touched the crack of my ass, and with the slippery shampoo running down my back and onto my behind, I wiggled against him, just enough to push his cock between my cheeks.

"That's nice, Roxy. Very nice," he murmured thickly, pulsing against me with a slow rhythm.

With one hand on the wall, I took the other and

reached behind myself to place it on his hip and pull him closer against me.

His breath was coming deep and raspy. "You know, Roxy, if you keep doing that, I'm going to come all over your pretty little bottom."

That did it. My free hand flew down between my legs and to my engorged clit, which was not taking a moment longer of being ignored. I bent at the waist to push harder against Silas, and when his groans grew, I rubbed my clit faster until my own orgasm built. Just as I felt thick streams of Silas's cum squirt between my ass cheeks, I began to shake from head to toe. He wrapped a strong arm around my waist to keep me upright, and I wilted into a massive orgasm.

That's what I wished had happened, anyway.

And now I was sitting in class, facing off with someone who wanted to fuck up my already-fucked up life.

"Paloma—" I started to say.

But she cut me off. Because bitches like her were smart that way. "Tell me Roxy, were you cleaning *his* house just like you do the hotel? Are you his new *maid*?" she taunted.

I clenched my fists. I wasn't against popping her one in the mouth, but my lifetime of growing up in a slightly rough neighborhood had taught me to use violence as a last resort. I didn't need an assault charge on my record along with all the other shit going down in my life.

But that didn't mean my muscles weren't quivering

to give her what she deserved. Who knew what the fuck she saw me doing? I didn't care. It was none of her goddamn business.

"I don't know what I ever did to you, Paloma, but please go fuck yourself." I opened my notebook with a loud *slap* on my desk.

Her eyes bulged, distorting her otherwise perfect face. It figured. People like Paloma weren't used to being called out. It hurt their feelings. They didn't like it.

But I did. A lot.

She stormed off to her seat somewhere in the back of the room with all the other beautiful people, and I returned to thinking about my imaginary architectural professor lover.

Just for fun, of course. I'd never go for an arrangement like Birdie or Jessa. But I could still have fun dreaming. And masturbating.

Silas Fox was his full name. Thirty-two years old. Spent his first years out of college working at a top architectural firm. Didn't like the long hours, and turned to academia.

Lucky for me.

But my thoughts were interrupted by giggling coming from the back of the room. I didn't turn around. I didn't need to. Paloma and her minions were undoubtedly up to no good.

Cripes, I'd sneaked out of the house that morning so stealthily, jogging to the other side of the street and then down the block just to put some distance between myself and the professors' house.

What did Paloma do, spy on him? And why did she give a shit anyway?

I never should have gone there. What had I been thinking?

And imagine the freaky coincidence of seeing Silas working on a project my father was undoubtedly part of. I'd nearly choked on my coffee right there.

But still, I'd not done anything wrong. Right?

After the humiliation of telling Arrow's class about my pathetic life, and then having my car break down, I hadn't been thinking at all. It was like my brain had run out of gas. Arrow had offered to take charge for a moment, and I let him.

And look at me now.

I could have been in any one of the houses in that neighborhood a few blocks from campus, for all Paloma knew. The location was convenient to campus, and I could see why Arrow had bought a home there. But I was staying away from now on. I didn't need more trouble in my life.

My business analytics professor finally showed up. In seconds, he'd connected his laptop to the projector, sharing the usual charts and spreadsheets that made my eyes cross, which were strangely interesting to me that morning.

Escaping class before Paloma could catch up to me, I took my newfound energy right over to the bursar's office to talk to them again about my tuition bill. I wasn't going to accept that someone in their third year like me, who'd always paid on time and earned decent grades, could just be cast aside.

There had to be something they could do.

"Student ID please," the clerk droned when my turn came.

He'd tried to threaten my optimism with his shitty tone. He'd better not try that again.

I held my chin high as I stared him down through a thick glass partition that reminded me of the DMV.

"I need some help with—" I started to say as he scanned my ID and clicked around on his keyboard.

"YOUR TUITION IS UNPAID," he bellowed, grabbing the attention of not only all his coworkers but also the other students waiting their turns.

Now I understood why there was a glass partition protecting his weaselly little face.

My stomach churned as all the feelings welled up inside me, including a smidgeon of fear. But I didn't do fear.

It wasn't my thing. I chased that bitch right away.

I did *pissed off* pretty well, though.

My old friend anger coursed through my veins,

giving me the power to take on shit the way urban legend had it that a desperate mother barehandedly lifted a car off her trapped child.

Watch out fuckers.

I was pissed about a lot of things, not least of which was being treated like a deadbeat by some university paper-pusher.

I took a deep breath. I wasn't going to lose my shit. At least not yet. "Thank you. I realize my tuition is *unpaid*. That's why I'm here. To talk to you about my situation."

He looked at me over the top of his glasses. "There isn't much we can do about UNPAID TUITION."

Fuck me. Is that how they trained clerks in the bursar's office? Humiliate the students! That will get rid of them!

Not today, Satan.

I tapped my foot, hoping it would bleed off some energy, which was rapidly becoming dangerous. Deadly, even.

It didn't help. "Do you get some sort of joy repeating my tuition payment status loudly, so everyone around us can hear it and join in my misery? Is that FUN FOR YOU?" I asked, my voice growing louder with each word.

His head snapped back on his shoulders and his lips drew together like he'd sucked a lemon. "Miss, if you raise your voice at me, I'll have to ask you to leave."

The run and hide tactic, popular with all useless people.

I wanted to kill him. Well, not kill. Maybe maim. Yes, maim would be nice. And satisfying. But since that was not a viable option, I lowered my voice.

"I'm here to ask whether I can have an extension on paying my tuition bill. My family is having financial problems right now."

I didn't share that my father might be a criminal. I didn't think it would garner much sympathy.

I continued. "You can see my tuition is fifty percent paid. That is my share. My parents were to pay the other half, but now can't. I need time to come up with the money. But I will find a way. Can I just stay in school in the meantime?"

He drew in a long, tired breath.

Maybe he heard sob stories like mine every day. But I didn't care. My story was *my* fucking story, and I needed a fucking solution.

"We have payment plans," he said, as if we'd reached a detente.

I nodded. "Yes, I know that. Right now I'm working as a hotel maid. I'm not sure the money I make could cover the payments."

He shook his head sadly, and for a moment I almost felt as sorry for him as he seemed like he was for me. "It's tough. Paying for college. I know. That's why I work here. Reduced tuition," he said in a lowered voice.

"Really? Are you guys hiring?" I asked hopefully.

"Nope. We're all full up. But you can keep checking back."

I nodded. "Fine. Can you set up the payment plan?

And I'll see if I can figure something out, some way to pay it."

He clicked on his keyboard. "Sure. Look for a letter with details."

"Um, can you email it to me? My parents' house is being foreclosed on."

Now the pity really filled his face. I wanted to chafe against it, but I needed it to work for me.

He nodded with a grave expression. "Yes. Will do."

I walked out of there convincing myself I'd made some progress. I had to believe that. Otherwise, I'd never get out of bed again.

8

BAIRD PRIESTLY

"Do you live here, too?"

It was always disconcerting to see someone out of context. And in that moment, I was about as unnerved as I had been in a long time.

I took a step backward into the house, staring out the open front door.

"Mr. Priestly? I mean, Baird. Are you… okay?"

I stared back at a face I knew perfectly well, which my surroundings told me I didn't know at all. The face didn't belong here, at my house, asking whether I lived there in addition to anybody else.

This was my home, and having a student show up on my front step was… bizarre.

"Ugh, yes. I live here," I stumbled.

Roxy Vandenberg smiled politely, showing off that gap in her teeth that made her so unique. "Well. You live with Arrow and Silas. That's… interesting," she said.

How did she know those guys lived here?

What the hell was going on?

"Can I… can I ask what you're doing here, Roxy?" I asked, forcing my own smile.

"Yes. I believe Arrow has my car. Or at least knows where it is."

Okay. Things were going from strange to fucking insane.

"How would he know where your car is, Roxy?"

She launched into the story of presenting her financial problems to his class. That made total sense. And when he walked her to her car after class, it wouldn't start.

Then, for some reason that was beyond my understanding, he brought her here and set her up in the guest room.

"And how do you know Silas, Roxy?" I asked.

She pointed to her hair. "He loaned me shampoo this morning," she said, like it all made sense.

And I guess it did. In some faraway universe where it was okay for students to spend the night in their professor's homes.

Over her shoulder, I waved to neighbors walking their dog, who were looking quizzically at the young woman at my door. They, like everyone else in the neighborhood, knew we three guys were all with the university. And it wouldn't be that much of a jump to figure the pretty young woman at our door was a student.

Not a good look.

I stepped back and gestured for her to get inside, away from prying eyes. "So you're here for your car?" I asked.

She nodded. "You know, I didn't get a good look at this place last night. Or this morning, for that matter. It's gorgeous. Really, really nice," she said, doing a three-sixty-degree turn to take everything in.

"Yeah, thanks. It's all Arrow. He has great taste. Or whoever he hired had great taste."

"Coffee?" I asked, unsure of what to say next.

What else could I do in such a situation?

"No. No thank you."

I gestured toward a chair for her and grabbed one myself. "Arrow and I became friends through my volunteer work with the Boys Club. He had this house and I lived in a little apartment, so he invited me to stay. Silas, who's waiting for his own house to be built is also involved—"

"Right. He's designing the apartments in the old movie theater," she said, fidgeting.

I sat back in my chair. "It's a cool project. I'm really excited about it."

"I used to go to that theater when I was a kid," she said, digging her fingernails into her palms.

What the fuck was going on here?

"You're a local girl?" I asked.

She looked around nervously. "Yes, but not from this neighborhood. The other side of the tracks, as they say."

Now that my initial surprise at having a student

show up at my door had dissipated, I quickly remembered what was so charming about this one. Even though she was going through some shit, she was still a refreshing bit of sunniness. Well, at least when she wasn't a ball of nerves.

"Would you like to see the theater some time? It's pretty rough right now, and you'd have to wear a hard hat," I offered.

But she waved away my idea. "It would be cool to see the place, sure. It's been so long. I could point out where my friends and I used to sneak in, and where I had my first kiss."

Why wasn't I surprised Roxy had her first kiss at a classic old movie theater?

She looked away dreamily.

Easier times, I supposed.

"Okay," I said, slapping my hand on the kitchen table. "We'll make it happen. Now, tell me what's up since I saw you at the faculty club with Arrow."

She sucked in her breath and grimaced.

"Well, I did that thing for Arrow's class. And I went to the bursar's office today to talk about a payment plan. In fact, they were going to email me an agreement or something. Let's see if I've received it yet."

She began to rustle around in her backpack, and pulled out her phone.

"Not sure I can make payments on what I make cleaning at the hotel, but I am curious to see how it would all work."

She pressed several buttons on her phone, frowned, and began jamming them even harder.

"Your phone battery die?" I asked.

She shook her head slowly. "No, it was fine last time I checked it. The cell service seems to be… down"

Then, a pink tinge crept across her face, and the forlorn expression she'd worn the day in my office when she'd started to cry, returned.

"No. No, no, no. This can't be."

She stared at her blank phone screen, then slammed it down and put a hand over her face. "Oh my god. My service is turned off. That's why my phone isn't fucking working. I mean, I can get wifi. But no calls or texts or data."

Oh Christ.

"What's up with your phone service?" I asked, watching a vein on the side of her neck begin to pulse.

"I'm on a plan with the rest of my family. Everyone's phone was probably shut off at the same time. My dad stopped paying bills and things, but it never occurred to me that would include our cell service. I'm so stupid," she said in a shaking voice. "I am so fucked. Just so fucked."

I reached to pat her back and she tensed like she was about to break into pieces. So I just kept smoothing my hand over her hooded sweatshirt. It was when her bottom lip began to quiver that I pulled her to me and wrapped my arms around her. I knew I shouldn't have. But I couldn't help it.

I was Roxy, not so long ago. I mean, I wasn't lost in

the arms of my academic advisor, but I was flat broke and about as down and out as you could get. A stroke of luck in the way of a kind, mentoring professor saved my ass. But until that happened, I'd been beyond forlorn about my future.

Not a good place to be. And that's where Roxy was just then.

She nestled her head into the crook of my neck and with a small turn of my head I buried my nose in her hair.

Again, off limits. Again, I didn't care.

She smelled damn good, even if it was Silas's shampoo.

I ran my hand down the back of her head. I just had to touch those beautiful blonde locks.

And they were soft. So soft.

She sighed, I hoped signaling she was done with her mini-breakdown, and when she pulled her head off my chest and looked up at me, our lips met.

It wasn't planned. It happened as spontaneously as I'd thrown my arms around her.

But it also felt natural.

I put my hands on either side of her face and pulled her to me because I wanted more. A lot more.

I was barely settled into my campus office when there was a knock on my door.

"Come in," I called, powering up my laptop.

"Hello, Mr. Priestly."

Why students called me Mr. Priestly instead of Baird was beyond me. But breaking them of the habit was near impossible.

"Oh, hello, Paloma. How are you?" I asked.

She slunk in and plopped into the chair opposite my desk, making herself at home, smiling at me and twisting one of her earrings. She was a beautiful woman, no doubt. But she looked like nearly all the other pretty blondes at Wellshire. It was amazing what Daddy's money could buy in the looks department. "Well," she said, sniffing, "I was fine until I failed an exam."

She thrust a paper in front of me marked with a big, red F, as if I might not believe her without proof.

Why the hell had she come to me with her poor grade?

"Why do you think you got an F, Paloma?" I asked.

She rolled her eyes and shrugged. "Well, I studied. The professor just asked questions on stupid stuff."

Stupid stuff. Yeah…

"Did you talk to him or her? What do you plan to do about it?"

But all she did was look around my office, seemingly uninterested in the poor grade she came in to talk to me about.

Then she leaned forward in her seat, tapping her manicured nails on my desk. "Hey, I saw that townie redneck coming out of your house this morning," she said with an expression that looked like she'd smelled something bad.

What the fucking fuck?

Had someone just kicked me in the stomach? Because it sure felt like it. There was so much that was fucked up about that statement.

And she knew it. She stared at me, expectantly, waiting to see what I was going to say.

With no change in my expression or tone, I didn't miss a beat. "*Townie redneck?* Is that what you call someone who grew up here?"

She huffed. "Well, not everyone who grew up here. Just the ones from the other side of town. You know."

Yeah. I didn't know.

Fuck me. How could I get this woman out of my office without giving her an actual kick in the ass?

"Paloma, was there anything else you wanted to talk about today?"

A slim smile grew across her face which, if you'd asked me before she'd come into my office with her trivial gripes, I would have said was lovely. But since she'd so blatantly displayed who she really was, I found her face obscene. Ugly. Disgusting.

She got to her feet and sauntered to the door. "Nope. That's all," she quipped.

"Well, hey, good luck with that grade. I think you'd better discuss with your professor the 'stupid stuff' he saw fit to test you on. It might be something worth learning."

She scowled at me, which didn't make her look any better, and slammed the door behind her.

Redneck townie? At my house?

What was that little guttersnipe going after?

Oh, that I could wring her scrawny little neck.

Sometimes I wondered if academic advising was for me. I'd been sure it was for so many years, but I had so much trouble summoning compassion for the spoiled, uncommitted students who had no appreciation for their privilege.

But if it weren't my current profession, I'd never have met someone like Roxy. Nor would I have had the opportunity to kiss her.

9

ROXY VANDENBERG

"HOUSEKEEPING!"

At the manager's request, I had stopped hollering to announce my arrival to our hotel guests. But I still called it out as assertively as possible. I just didn't want to walk in on any more naked people.

When I didn't hear anything after several raps with my knuckles, I pulled the master card key out of my pocket, and prepared to slide it in the door locking mechanism. But before I did, I leaned my ear against the door, just to be sure. I could have sworn I heard a little rustling from inside.

And just as I met the cold door, the room erupted in moans and groans so loud they nearly split my eardrum.

Okay. So these folks were busy.

"I'll come back later," I called, thanking god I hadn't just blown into the room.

Seriously. Why can't people just use their Do Not Disturb signs?

Then someone from inside the room actually answered me. That never happened.

"We'll be right out! Five more minutes!" a woman called.

I looked at my watch. I could hang out for five minutes. I was ahead of schedule, anyway, working by myself that day, which was actually faster than working with Lolo. She talked so much we usually barely finished in time.

So, with the hallway to myself, I leaned against the wall and out of habit pulled out my phone.

Shit.

Funny how certain actions were such habits. I actually had to look at my missed calls for a minute before I realized I hadn't had any in a couple days. Because I had no cell service.

That happens when you don't pay the bill.

So, without an electric babysitter to entertain me, my thoughts worked their way back to the kiss I'd gotten from Baird.

Poor guy. I'd broken down in front of him twice now. He was going to think I was a bigger loser than I was. If that were possible.

I didn't know what it was about him, but the emotions just seemed to flow when he was around. I guess it was the sense of comfort I got from him. He knew my situation. He'd had his own set of challenges.

And it just felt so good to know someone had overcome their shit, and made it.

I wanted to make it.

This whole tuition thing was just a set-back.

And to be honest, if it hadn't happened, I would never have kissed Baird, heard Arrow pleasuring himself, or given Silas an eyeful of my birthday suit in the bathroom.

I wanted to deny it, but a little tickle kicked in *down there*, and I squirmed in my all-black maid's outfit. It wasn't helped by the moans coming from the room I was waiting to clean.

Not that I really had anything going on with any of the guys, but cripes, I'd had three encounters, all within about twenty-four hours of each other, with some of the most handsome men I'd ever laid eyes on.

After Baird had stopped kissing me, he'd offered me a ride to work. I didn't say a word the entire way.

Carless. Phoneless. I was a sorry sight. Not even sure why he wanted to kiss me to begin with.

The noises on the other side of the hotel room door were getting louder. Hopefully that meant they were nearly finished.

On one hand, I couldn't believe I'd kissed my academic advisor, spent the night at my professor's house, and let another see me naked. I wasn't usually one to throw caution to the wind. I liked plans. I liked it when things went the way I expected them to.

But things had gotten so unpredictable lately, maybe all my planning had been a stupid waste of time.

You think you know where you're going and in an instant everything can get derailed. So, why the hell shouldn't I go for it?

Even if the Palomas of the world were full of endless, cruel, contemptuous judgment?

Fuck her. She knew nothing about my life, and yet had the nerve to try and make trouble for me. I'd get to the bottom of why she had such a hard-on for giving me a hard time.

A person can put up with only so much shit, and I was pretty sure I'd reached my lifetime maximum.

Seriously. If someone as much as looked at me wrong, they'd be taking their life into their hands. That's about where I was with things.

The door to the room I'd been waiting on suddenly jerked open, and the couple that had been having such a good time bounded out looking fresh and happy. They only briefly glanced my way, grabbed each other's hands, and hurried down the hallway giggling.

I wanted tell them no need to be embarrassed. More power to them. At least that's what I was thinking before I got a look at the condition they'd left their room in.

The sheets had come completely off the bed. There was a half-empty bottle of lube on the nightstand next to a colorful magazine called *Pegging*. And a huge strap-on dildo sat on a towel on the bathroom sink, where it was quietly drying.

At least they washed their sex toys.

When I'd finished my cleaning rounds, I returned to my locker, where there was a note taped to the door.

You got a call from an Arrow Menken. He asks that you call him.

Wow. A phone message. Just like in the old days, before cell phones.

"Can I borrow the office phone?" I asked my manager.

Barney looked up from the spreadsheet he was pouring over. "Um, yeah. Okay. You lose your cell?"

"Something like that," I murmured, dialing Arrow's number.

"Hello?" he answered.

"Hi, Arrow, it's Roxy."

"Oh, hey," he said in an animated voice. "Are you done with work yet?"

"Yes, I am," I said, hoping he'd hurry since I was standing under Barney's watchful eye.

"Great. I've just ordered an Uber for you. It should arrive at the front of the hotel in five minutes. See you in a bit."

Well, that was a surprise. Maybe my car was done, which would be awesome. I wasn't sure how long it would take to pay Arrow back for the repairs, but I'd find a way.

Right?

When the Uber dropped me off, I hustled up to Arrow's door because I didn't want to give that creep Paloma any more ammo for fucking with me—if that were possible. And as soon as I rang the doorbell, he answered.

"Hey, Roxy, come on in."

He was so friendly I wasn't sure whether to greet him with a hug and kiss, or just shake his hand.

So, I just didn't do either.

"Thank you for sending the Uber," I said. "And thank you for letting me spend the night…"

I didn't finish. Instead, I buried my face in my backpack like I was looking for something, in order to hide my blushing face. A white heat ran through me as I thought back to listening to Arrow pleasure himself, especially when he called out my name. Thank god I'd been silent through my own play time. The last thing I needed was for him to hear *me*. I couldn't bear that level of embarrassment.

As I wondered whether I should mention my car, or wait for him to, he smiled, his blue eyes shining in the late afternoon sun. He ran his fingers through his hair, raking a couple locks off his forehead, and led me to the kitchen, where a giant spread of Chinese take-out had been laid out.

My stomach instantly growled, and I realized I'd not eaten all day. I could normally swipe a cookie or two from the kitchen, but the usual chef wasn't there to slip me anything.

I didn't want to assume I was invited, but damn if

Arrow's feast didn't look amazing. He probably had any number of friends—particularly women—he might have invited over, and from the amount of food he'd ordered, it seemed he was expecting a crowd.

I'd just grab my car and get the hell out.

"Oh, that looks great, I'm starving," Baird said, joining us.

I returned to fishing through my backpack to hide another red face. I didn't need to be reminded of his delicious lips just then. Or ever.

"Hey, glad you're here Roxy, we can finally sit down to eat. The smell of this stuff is killing me. It's gonna be so good," he said, pulling out a chair for me.

Okay then. I guess I was invited to dinner.

I grabbed some chopsticks, still not sure why I'd been invited to dinner, aside from the obvious errand of picking up my car. An errand that didn't usually include a meal.

But I wasn't complaining.

"Mmmm," I said. "This wonton soup is amazing."

Arrow reached across the table for potstickers. "This is from my favorite Chinese place."

"Oh man," Baird said, jumping to his feet. "Almost forgot the beer."

He returned with a six pack of Tsingtao, popped the cap off one, and passed it to me.

Oh my god. I was in heaven.

"This is delicious. I haven't had a beer in ages, and with all that's going on in my life, it is such a treat to sit down and eat something not from the dining hall."

They paused their eating for a second, nodded, and got back to their chopsticks.

"And… it's especially nice to share with a couple of… um, you know, nice guys." As lame as my thanks sounded, I forced myself to look at each guy for several seconds. As embarrassed as I was by everything—and I meant everything—I needed to convey my appreciation.

"It's so… kind, the way you're helping me out. I don't know how I can ever begin to thank you."

There. I'd said it.

"Well, Roxy," Arrow said, setting down his chopsticks, "we figured you needed to eat. And, your car is being repaired as we speak. So, we're happy to help you out."

Wonton soup dribbled down my chin. "Really? Um, how much is it? Because if I can't afford it—"

But Arrow waved away my concerns. "I've got it covered for you, Roxy."

Huh?

"What do you mean—?"

He cut me off again. "I've already paid for it. I'm happy to do it. I like… helping deserving people."

Holy shit. Did I have a sugar daddy?

Or daddies?

Was I headed for the life Birdie and Jessa had found? Love with their professors?

Ugh. That was stupid. Just plain stupid. These guys were just helping me get on my feet. Nothing more.

"I'll… I'll pay you back as soon as I can. I mean, it might be a while. But I'm good for it," I said.

Arrow nodded. "I am sure you are. Your credit is good with me."

"Why are you helping me like this?" I blurted.

There was no other way to put it. I had to know.

Arrow shot Baird a glance, then leaned on the table in my direction. "That's a good question, Roxy. I guess… I guess I know what it's like to be where you are. And I know that with a little boost—or maybe a big one—you can get out of this rut. It might not feel like it right now, but all this… shit going on in your life will pass. You will come out on top. I know it."

Holy shit. That was about the nicest thing anyone ever said to me.

My throat got a little tight, but this time I wasn't going to cry. I was so over that shit. So, I held my head up. "I'm so lucky. Lucky to have you guys on my side. You're correct, right now it feels like there is no way out of this… slump. I want to believe you. I really do."

Baird reached across the table and took my hand. "I'd be skeptical if I were you, too."

And with that, he rose from his side of the table, pulled me to my feet, and kissed me even more passionately than he had that morning.

Right in front of Arrow.

Who I stole a glance at, sitting back in his chair, grinning.

Jesus. Was this a *thing* for these guys? Had they done this before?

Kissing a down and out little undergrad, with the other one watching?

But I didn't want to seem like I was complaining, because the whole thing was actually hot as fuck.

Two guys, quite different from each other with Baird's hippy vibe and Arrow's quiet, proper one, had invited me over. And now it looked like we might have some fun.

What if Silas walked in?

But I didn't have time to worry about that.

"Tell me, Roxy," Arrow said.

Baird and I stopped kissing long enough to look his way.

"How many men have you been with?"

A loud gasp escaped my throat. "What?"

He did not really just ask that, did he? And now, he'd gotten up from his seat and was working his way over.

"Yeah, Roxy, I'd like to know," Baird added.

My eyes darted between the two of them. "Wh.. why?" I stammered.

He shrugged. "Just nosy that way. But a woman as beautiful as you must have many suitors. In fact, I'm surprised you were free tonight to come over."

Was he kidding? Did he really think I had guys knocking my door down?

Arrow came up behind me and placed his hands on my shoulders, leaning close enough to bury his face in my hair. With Baird standing right in front of me, watching my reaction, I was effectively sandwiched between the two men.

And while I clenched my fists to bleed off some of my nervousness, I couldn't think of another place I'd rather be. I wanted to feel good and forget my problems, if only for a little while.

"Fou… five," I mumbled.

Baird's head snapped back. "Five guys? That's all?" he asked, incredulously.

Well shit. How many guys had other twenty-one-year-old college students been with? Was five that bad?

I knew 'my number' was more than Birdie, but less than Jessa. Although, all bets were off now since they had their professor 'harems.'

They laughed when I called them harems.

But I thought it was the perfect name.

"Hey, gorgeous," Arrow whispered in my ear after he'd run his lips down the side of my neck, "how'd you like to retire to another room? My bedroom?"

10

ARROW MENKEN

Holy Christ.

I had Roxy Vandenberg in my bedroom.

Fucking hot.

And Baird, too.

It wasn't the first time I'd bedded a student. Not that I'd brag about it. When a college professor was surrounded by vibrant, beautiful, young women all day long, it was natural that attractions built. But I wasn't predatory about it like I'd seen another colleague of mine behave. In fact, that guy was no longer with the university. They'd kicked his ass out when he'd gotten a girl pregnant and unceremoniously dumped her.

Seems the girl's father, who was an alum of Wellshire, didn't think much of that sort of behavior.

Couldn't blame him.

Some of the girls I'd known just wanted to spread their legs for a better grade. I mean, if someone feels like the only currency she has is her pussy, fine. No judgment. It just didn't turn me on.

Now, a student like Roxy, where the attraction was mutual, was a different story. Hell, we were all consenting adults, and while the folks in charge might say there was a power imbalance between a student and professor, I wasn't entirely sure I bought that. I'd known a couple smart, strong women over the years who knew what they wanted and were the least exploitable people I'd ever met. They owned their sexuality like the self-possessed women they were. One of them had been in my life for nearly a year until she graduated and moved away. I would always wish her the best.

As soon as Roxy, Baird, and I got to my bedroom, I pointed to an oversized easy chair in my sitting area, which I often used to read or watch TV.

Or jerk off.

I pointed at Baird. "Why don't you go sit in that chair over there, buddy?"

He looked at me knowingly. Yeah, I was hooking his ass up. I wasn't about cock-blocking. Roxy was hot for us. It was written all over her. There'd be plenty to go around.

I turned to her, running my fingers through her silky hair, and pulled her to me for a kiss. Her lips were soft and pliant under mine, and her warm breath and small sigh got me so hard I had to readjust myself in my trousers.

My effort did not go unnoticed. She pulled back

and smiled at me as she lifted her hoodie over her head and threw it to the floor.

Underneath, she was wearing a white cropped T-shirt with an outline of Betty White on it. And no bra.

"Who doesn't love Betty White?" I asked, my hands flying to the bare flesh of her belly, warm and smooth, and marked by a tiny belly button piercing.

"Do you know how beautiful you are?" I asked, holding her face so she couldn't turn away.

"Thank you," she said quietly.

"So modest, isn't she?" Baird called from the chair where he was sitting.

I tilted her chin up and her eyes met mine. "You've been told that before, haven't you? That you're beautiful?" I asked.

She shrugged. "Yeah. I have."

"Good. Because I want you to remember it."

I released her face and took her hand, leading her to my seating area.

"Now, I'd like to watch you kiss Baird," I said, pushing her in his direction.

Her eyes widened, and she giggled, walking toward him slowly.

He looked up, admiring the hell out of her, and pulled her down to straddle him. I sat back in the easy chair next to them, and watched.

Baird ran his hands up and under her shirt, where he found her bare tits. Breaking their gaze, he lifted her shirt and pulled her to his mouth. He circled one of her nipples with his tongue while kneading her other breast.

"You like that, baby?" he whispered.

She arched, dropping her head back and pushing her breast harder into his mouth. I couldn't remember when I had seen a more beautiful sight.

When Baird had had enough of her tits, he yanked at the button on her blue jeans, and lowered the zipper far enough to reach his fingers inside.

Grabbing his shoulders, Roxy ground her pelvis against his hand.

Fucking hot. I'd watched for long enough.

I got up and pressed my hard cock against Roxy's back, reaching around for her tits while Baird continued, his hand in her pants, working her pussy.

"Such a pretty girl," I murmured.

I signaled Baird, and he pulled his hand out of her pants and released her.

I guided her to her feet, and she climbed off Baird, wobbly legs and all, and turned her to face me.

"You good, darling? You feeling good?" I asked as she caught her balance.

Her eyes, which had been closed, fluttered open. "Yes, Arrow. I've never felt this good in my entire life." She leaned forward to place her lips on mine, straining to overcome our height difference.

As we kissed for the first time, Baird got to his feet. Now that he was behind her, he shimmied her jeans down and helping her step out of them. There she stood before us, with her slim hips and flawless skin, her breasts tipped with erect nipples.

"Would you like to be fucked, beautiful?" I whispered in her ear.

If she hesitated even for a moment, all bets were off. Hers was the only lead that would be followed.

But to my pleasure, she nodded and whispered back. "I do, Arrow. But who's gonna fuck me? You or Baird?"

She tilted her head, and I pushed a long strand of hair off her forehead.

I looked at Baird over her shoulder. He continued pulling, and then soothing, her nipples. "Baird will fuck you, baby. I will watch."

Yeah, I liked to watch. I was a freak that way.

She gave me a little smile and turned to face Baird, leaning just enough to press her ass against my raging hard-on.

Christ, she was going to kill me.

She pulled Baird's shirt off over his head and unbuckled his belt. She paused long enough to lay a nice kiss on his lips, and then made quick work of getting his jeans and boxers off, where they puddled on the floor. He took her hand and moved back to the chair where he'd been sitting, and pulled her down to straddle his hips again.

He quickly sheathed himself with a condom he'd pulled from his jeans pocket, and held his cock straight up to wait for her to lower herself on it.

I rubbed myself through my pants, barely able to

contain my excitement. The beautiful Roxy was about to get fucked, and I was right behind her with a perfect view of her spreading pussy and ass.

"Ugh!" she groaned when Baird pulled her down on his cock.

I watched him slide in and out, her pussy lips stretching to accommodate his engorged dick. I quietly moved up behind her to put my hands on her pretty ass cheeks, gently pulling them apart to get a better view of her rosebud asshole.

With a wet finger, I stroked her there and she puckered tightly. But she must have liked it because she ground down on Baird's dick so hard he grunted from the sensation.

"Fuck!" he groaned, gripping her hips and pistoning her up and down.

That's when I pressed a finger into her ass up to the knuckle and she started bucking like crazy. I never imagined she'd have a reaction like that, and pressed my finger deeper.

Her head flew forward and then back as an orgasm crashed into her, leaving her tightening on my finger and probably Baird's dick, too.

With a great roar, Baird came, pinning Roxy down hard as a second orgasm rocked her.

I removed my finger from her behind, and lifted her from Baird's lap. She was too weak to walk to the bed, so I scooped her into my arms and lay her down, where she promptly turned over on her side with a wicked little smile, looking up at me one last time before she closed her eyes and dozed.

"Is she still here?"

Leaving Roxy snoozing in my room, Baird and I had grabbed more beers and lowered ourselves into the hot tub in my backyard. Silas joined us five minutes later when he'd returned from his last class.

"Yeah, man," Baird said. "She conked out on Arrow's bed. Fucking beautiful, all that blonde hair spread over her pillow…"

Okay. Somebody was smitten.

But he wasn't the only one.

Silas's eyes widened and he nodded approvingly. "Well done, my man. And I'm guessing you were both present for your fun little session."

It wasn't the first time I'd shared a woman with Baird. And now Silas probably felt left out. But he was a big boy and could make his own good times.

"So, dude," Baird said to Silas, "I understand you met Roxy the other morning."

He laughed and shook his head. "I sure did. She startled the shit out of me. In a good way. You say she's going through a rough time? She's the one you had present to your class, huh?"

I nodded. "Yeah. And they loved her. They were so

excited to have a real-world case study to consider, even though most of their suggestions were useless."

I wanted to do more to help her.

Fuck, I could just offer to pay her tuition. I lived comfortably enough to do that, given the lucrative years I spent on Wall Street. But I liked keeping the level of assets I'd accumulated private. Not even Baird or Silas, two of my closest friends, knew the full extent of what I had.

"I gotta tell you guys," Silas started, "I was impressed as hell by her. She's not only good-looking, but she was very curious about the movie theater project, which I had open on my laptop. She took a look, made a couple suggestions, and no word of a lie, had an idea for improving the design. I was blown away. Hey, did you guys know her dad's a contractor or something?"

"No kidding?" Baird said. "Maybe that's where she gets her sense of space. She's a smart cookie. I wish I could do more to help her, too."

"You're doing a lot buddy, believe me," Silas said. "Hey guys, on another note, I got an interesting call today."

"Yeah? From whom?" Baird asked.

"From a firm. An architectural firm. My old one. They want me to come back to work for them."

Holy shit.

"Well, I'm not surprised. You're good at what you do," Baird said, sucking back the last of his beer.

"What are you going to do?" I asked. "I mean, you

should consider it. Compare it to your work here at the university. Even if you don't take it, it's always good to consider options."

He nodded. "Yup. I agree. The only thing is that should I take it, I'd have to move across the country."

Damn. No one wanted that. But if he got to know Roxy as Baird and I had, he'd never leave town. And his turn would come soon.

11

ROXY VANDENBERG

"How'd you sleep?"

I bolted up in bed, initially unsure of where I was, and found Arrow standing in the doorway of what I quickly realized was his bedroom.

I covered myself to the neck with his fluffy down comforter and squinted in the morning light. "Holy crap. I slept like the dead."

Without the usual noise of the dorm, where people yelled and slammed doors at all hours of the night, I fell into the kind of sleep I hadn't known in… I didn't know how long. Of course it helped that I'd just had my brains fucked out, too.

Arrow gave me his usual shy smile and took a couple steps into the room.

I liked that. It was as if he wanted to give me a little space. Not completely descend on me. But it was, after all, his bedroom.

Where the hell had he slept?

I loved that he was a secret perv. All preppy and proper on the outside, with his expensive shoes and monogrammed everything, standing before his classes spouting dry financial theory.

But behind closed doors, the man was a freak and I had a feeling we'd barely even scratched the surface. First, there was his inclination to 'watch,' and then his affinity for butt play.

I just couldn't.

And that hungry, wanting ache between my legs, which had erupted into the most perfect orgasm of my life, just the night before?

Yup. It was back. I was all tingly and gooey down there and dammit, I had classes to get to.

"Sorry to have kicked you out of your bed. Where did you sleep?" I asked, yawning.

What was the protocol here? I needed to get my ass out of bed and get dressed, but right in front of Arrow? Granted, he'd seen me… in all my glory, but in the light of day, did I just walk around naked in front of him? Was that cool?

"I slept in the guest room where you slept the other night. In fact, the pillow still smelled like your hair."

Holy crap. He noticed what my hair smelled like.

Just then, Silas burst into the doorway. "Morning, Roxy. Hey, guys I'm heading to campus. Anyone need a ride?"

Like this was the most normal thing ever.

Silas adjusted the oversized black hipster glasses

that always seemed to slip down his nose, and looked between Arrow and me for an answer.

I raised my hand, as if I were in class.

Idiot.

"I'll take a ride, thank you. Just give me a couple minutes to get dressed," I said, looking directly at Arrow.

Silas disappeared, and Arrow backed out of the room. "See you downstairs," he said, with a nod of his head, pulling the door closed.

Good grief.

I'd just messed around with my finance professor and academic advisor. And it had been hot as shit.

Then, I'd spent the night, and their third roommate, another professor, offered me a ride to school as if my waking up naked in his home was totally normal.

My life had gone from bizarre to fucking out of control whacked.

I had nowhere to live, aside from crashing in Birdie and Jessa's dorm room, where I was really not even supposed to be, I had no car or phone, and I wasn't properly enrolled in my classes. I might end up doing a semester's-worth of class work, and if I were still in 'audit' status at the end of the term, I'd have earned no credit, and made no progress toward my degree.

Let's see. Had I left anything out of my sad sack life?

Wait. How could I forget? My father was likely a criminal, and I hadn't heard a word from my mother and little sister since our house had been taken.

Even the campus mean girl was after my ass.

Wow. When the universe decided to shit on me, it took a major dump.

Seemed like the only thing I had going for me was my hotel maid job. No complications there, aside from cleaning up after people indulging in 'afternoon delight.'

So as not to attract any additional bad juju—although I had no idea how my life could get more fucked up—once dressed, I tiptoed down the stairs with my shoes in my hand. If I made myself small and invisible, the cloud hanging over my head might lose sight of me.

And it seemed like that might just be working.

I found the three guys in the kitchen, chatting, and downing coffee. Baird handed one to me and I took a quick sip. I didn't want to make anyone late.

But they didn't seem to be in any sort of hurry.

It was the first time I'd been in a room with all three of them at once. And what a sight they were, all handsome, fit, smart, and accomplished, and all looking at *me*.

In what world did everything fall apart for a girl, who then finds herself spending time with three of the most beautiful specimens of maleness that ever existed?

Talk about whiplash.

Silas reached into his front pocket, and extended my phone. "We had your service turned back on. You're good to go. It won't be turned off again."

I took my phone, staring at it like it was some sort

of alien being. But it wasn't the phone that was unfamiliar. It was the grace of these men. Their kindness and generosity. It was new. And strange. And kind of uncomfortable.

I knew they felt for me, what with my shitty situation and all. Who knew, maybe they even felt sorry for me, and that was why they were being so nice.

Which didn't exactly feel good, but who was I to turn away a little kindness? I'd fallen into these guys' lives—or had they fallen into mine?—at a time when I most needed help, and they'd provided it to me in spades.

Not to mention shown me an incredible time behind closed doors.

I wasn't sure I deserved it, but I wasn't saying no.

After I powered it back on and my missed messages started downloading, I looked back up at them.

"I... I don't know what to say. I mean, thank you. So much. You've been so generous. I will pay you back for this. For everything."

Silas waved his hand at my suggestion. "Nonsense. We're happy to help someone deserving like you."

I ran and threw my arms around him, almost knocking off his nerd glasses. "Thank you, Silas."

Damn if he didn't smell good, and the way his strong arms wrapped around me sent shivers up my spine.

I released him and turned to Arrow. "Thank you so much," I said, pressing into his crunchy, starched shirt.

When it was Baird's turn, he held his arms open

with a huge grin. I fell into him without a word. Any awkwardness I'd anticipated never materialized. It was all so comfortable. And natural.

"You guys," I said, looking from one to the other, "are so… amazing. I… don't even know what to say."

Silas threw an arm around my shoulder. "Then say nothing, sweetie."

Arrow nodded. "Yeah, Roxy. Because we have something to tell you."

My heart skipped a beat.

"Um. Sounds serious," I said with a forced smile.

"You see," he continued, "we have an offer for you."

Ohgodohgodohgod.

I felt a trickle of boob sweat run down my chest, and while I casually held my coffee cup in one hand, I leaned against the kitchen counter, gripping it for all I was worth, with the other.

"Oh? An offer?" I croaked in a thin voice. "An offer for what?"

They nodded, nearly reducing me to dust.

Shit. Why hadn't I put on a little lip gloss or something?

"We're paying for your college," Arrow said.

I burst out with a strangled little laugh. "Ugh, you're paying for *what*?" I asked, certain I'd misheard them.

"Your tuition. If you agree to it, from hereon in, your tuition is covered. And you will live here, so we know you are safe."

A minute passed, and no one said anything. They

were waiting for me to speak. Hell, *I* was waiting for me to speak.

"W… why? Why would you do that?"

Was this some kind of sugar daddy arrangement?

Or was this hooking up with a professor thing all the rage? If you looked at Birdie and Jessa, then yes, it seemed like the case.

Baird held a finger up. "Very good question. We are going to employ you."

To do what? I was a freaking hotel maid.

My expression must have conveyed my confusion, because Silas jumped right in.

"Look, Roxy, when you were here the other day, your design suggestion for the movie theater was fantastic. I want to see if there's more where that came from."

I shook my head. "Oh no. I'm sure there's not. That was just a wild-assed guess. Beginner's luck." I laughed.

"It doesn't matter," he said, waving away my concerns. "I'm willing to give it a shot if you are. Baird could use admin help, filing and so forth, and Arrow needs help with his classes—preparing presentations, keeping track of assignments, and so forth."

While I wanted to just say no, and run out of the place, a small part of me let myself imagine this just might work.

Could it? Was it just batshit crazy, like every other aspect of my life?

Or was my luck taking a turn for the better?

Silas clapped his hands together and grabbed his

backpack. "Roxy, you are about as speechless as I thought you'd be. And that's okay. You need time to think over our offer. If your answer is no, we completely respect that. But right now, we all need to get to campus."

Everyone laughed as the tension broke, and we piled in Arrow's Range Rover. For once, I wasn't looking around, concerned about who might see me coming and going from the guys' house. I had done nothing wrong. I had nothing to be ashamed of. Paloma and her ilk could kiss my ass.

Baird joined me in the backseat, and while we rode to campus in silence, he caught me glancing his way. He tilted his head with a half-smile and winked, then reached across the seat and wrapped his pinky finger around mine.

That gesture, that touch, was so small and yet so big. It told me everything would be all right. I had some pretty big supporters on my side, and even if I didn't take their offer, I knew I could count on them for a moral boost when I needed it.

Which brought me to the question that I knew would occupy my thoughts for at least the rest of the day.

Should I take their offer?

Work for the three of them in exchange for having my bills paid?

With, what I assume, would be the occasional—or frequent?—fringe benefits that might come from living with the three most gorgeous men I'd ever known?

So many decisions to make, including the most important—what if I started to develop feelings for them? Would that bring the whole show down?

I was no expert, but I was pretty sure that wasn't how sugar daddy relationships worked. It was transactional. Feelings were not part of it.

But what did I know?

With my newly-turned on phone, I texted Jessa and Birdie.

EMERGENCY MEETING. NOW.

1 2

SILAS FOX

THERE WAS a knock at my office door, and the department chair stuck his head inside.

"Morning, Brad," I said.

All instructors, myself included, were required to schedule office hours at least once a week. There were no exceptions, which was the only reason I was here.

It was a silly requirement, really, because I saw my students multiple times a week in class and in studio. Any talks we needed to have, no matter what they were about, always happened there.

Regardless, I still had to sit for office hours, so I made the best of my time rather than looking at it as a waste. Although on this day, about all I could think about was the lovely Roxy, and what her being in our life—or not—might mean.

"Hey, Silas. Mind if we chat in my office?" Brad asked.

I'd been about to wave him into mine so we could

137

talk there, but okay. I stood to follow. One advantage of being in the office, I supposed, was face time with the boss.

I grabbed the chair opposite his desk.

"How are things with you, Brad? Busy?" I asked to make conversation.

Something about being summoned to his office felt like being called to the principal's office as a kid. Nothing good ever came of that.

He nodded deeply, settling behind his spotless desk. Folks in the architecture department were often a little different from academics in other parts of the university. Instead of the stereotypical 'absent-minded' professor whose office was in a shambles, we were a little more anal about our surroundings, and Brad was more so than almost anyone else I'd ever known. Aside from the giant iMac computer taking up half his desk, he had a framed picture that faced him so I couldn't see who was in it, and that's it.

"I'm well," he said, sitting back and crossing one leg at the knee. "But maybe I should ask *you* how things are."

He must have seen the puzzlement on my face, because he raised his eyebrows like I had news to share or something.

But I had nothing, at least not that I could think of. "I'm not sure what you mean. Is something up?"

He looked at me with the little smile I'd learned was common in the academic world. I didn't know if I would exactly call it passive-aggressive, but it was used by people when they were about to one-up you. In other words, they either had something on you, or knew something you didn't.

In the business world people were more direct. When I was a practicing architect, there was no time for beating around the bush or playing games. If someone liked something, they said so. If they didn't, they also said so. We had clients to please and more often than not, more work than there were hours in the day.

There was no time for fucking around.

Not so much in an academic setting.

It had all taken some adjustment on my part. I had to learn to smile when I felt like spitting, keep my real opinions to myself when it was called for, and fan the egos of my superiors, whether they deserved it or not.

I wished Brad would get on with whatever was on his mind.

But then a slight unease chilled me.

Did he know about Roxy? And was there an issue there? Being involved with her definitely skirted the edges of what people were and were not comfortable with. I got that. We might be consenting adults, but people did tend to focus on the power imbalance between professors and students.

In my opinion, however, a woman always held the power if she wanted to. And besides, in my case, Roxy wasn't my student.

After staring each other down for a moment, I

asked again. "What are you getting at, Brad? Could you please not beat around the bush?"

His eyes widened, almost imperceptibly, then went back to neutral. It always blew my mind how some people just couldn't deal with directness.

He sighed and tapped his keyboard, probably as more of a nervous tic than anything. "Well, Silas, I hear… that you're looking to leave. The university."

I didn't know whether to be relieved or irritated. I was grateful he wasn't asking about Roxy… but what the hell was he talking about, my wanting to leave my teaching position?

I leaned forward in my chair. "Brad, that's crazy. Where did you hear such a thing?"

He smirked. "Silas, you know I know a lot of people in the industry. There's little I don't hear about."

While I was getting pissed at his evasiveness, a lightbulb went off.

Okay. Got it now.

"Are you talking about my being offered a position at my old firm? Is that what this is about?"

He clasped his hands, relieved the information was out and on the table. "Yes. That's it exactly, Silas."

"Brad, they wanted to talk to me about coming back. They approached *me*. Not the other way around. I'm not sure how you took that to conclude I was looking to leave."

And even if I were looking to leave, what was the purpose of confronting me this way? I'd always thought this guy was an imperious douchebag, holding knowledge over people's heads and such. And now I knew he was.

He shrugged, throwing his hands up in the air. "I'm just telling you what I heard."

"Well, maybe you should consider the source," I said, fighting to keep the irritation out of my voice. "I have been approached about a position, like I just told you. No reason to hide that. But to conclude I'm looking to leave the university is a pretty big jump."

His shoulders slipped down a notch, seemingly chastened by my rational response. "Glad we cleared the air. But what are you thinking about the offer?"

I wasn't going to lie.

"Look, Brad, I love what I do here, teaching architecture. I am doing this because the firm life wasn't for me. But I'll listen to what they have in mind, because it would be crazy not to. Wouldn't you do the same?" I asked.

He considered me and nodded silently.

I went back to my office, unsure why I'd let Brad get under my skin. Perhaps it was because I really *was* considering the offer seriously, and was so conflicted about it. I'd worked hard to get where I was at Wellshire but I couldn't lie about missing working on the big projects. No one who'd trained as long as I had easily walked away from the excitement of seeing a design on paper—or on the computer, as things worked these days—to completion. It was hard to replace that rush with an academic setting, however rewarding it was to bring along the next generations of architects.

Fuck it. I had a lot to think about.

Not least of which was potentially leaving the house I was having built, and giving up my Boys Club volunteer work.

And Roxy.

Speaking of the lovely girl, I had some time to kill before my afternoon class and thought I might take her to lunch. Baird and Arrow had spent much more time with her, and I was looking forward to a little private time with her to get better acquainted.

I texted her newly-turned on cell. *Hey, beautiful. Lunch?*

She responded a minute later.

At the hotel. Working. Done in one hour.

See you soon. I'm taking you to lunch.

Cool!

That worked out well.

Except for one thing.

What the hell was she still doing working at the hotel? We guys had made her an offer that would permit her to leave that job behind. She couldn't possibly like working there, could she? Cleaning up hotel guest rooms?

Did this mean she wasn't accepting our offer?

Or that she was still thinking about it?

Only one way to find out.

I settled into a comfy lobby chair when I arrived at the hotel, and watched the crowd swirl around me. It had always fascinated me to see people traveling and what better place to be a fly on the wall and quietly observe than at a hotel?

Just as I was watching a big, loud man at the front desk have a meltdown because his preferred room was not available, two hands covered my eyes like a blindfold.

I immediately knew whose they were.

I turned to look up at Roxy, still in her maid's uniform, her hair in one long braid falling down her back.

Talk about hot. My girl dressed as a maid. A dozen dirty thoughts flooded my brain as I forced myself to try and focus.

"Hey, gorgeous," I said.

Her eyes brightened, and she ran her fingers down the side of my cheek. Then, remembering where we were, she anxiously looked around. "I gotta change so give me a couple minutes."

But as she started to walk away, I jumped to my feet and followed her. "Hey," I whispered after her.

"Yes?" she asked, looking around.

She must have a dick of a boss to be that nervous.

I pulled her into the empty elevator that had just opened next to us. "C'mon. Let's have some fun," I said, taking her hand and kissing it while the doors whirred shut.

Mischief splashed over her face and she seized my arm. "I have an idea. Follow me," she said, pressing the next floor. "But pretend you don't know me until we're alone."

Hell yeah.

I let her walk ahead of me, swinging her hips like a naughty girl, while I followed, pretending to do something on my phone. She slipped a card key through a lock, which clicked loudly. She motioned for me to follow, so I jogged to catch up, and she pulled the door closed behind us. Then, she propped an empty chair against the knob.

"What is this place?" I asked, my eyes adjusting to the dark. I couldn't see far, but what was right in front of me looked like folded up tables and stacked chairs.

"It's one of our ballrooms. When there's no event, it's used for storage. But look at this view," she said, taking my hand.

She was comfortable with me. Good sign.

I couldn't help but wonder what her thoughts were about the proposal we had made her, but now was not the time to ask.

We approached a large window extending the length of the room, which overlooked the hotel lobby and atrium.

"Wow," I said. "Gorgeous."

She stared out the window. "I never get tired of looking at this. It's so cool to spy on people."

"They can't see us up here?" I asked.

She looked at me with a playful grin. "Nope. The glass is mirrored on the other side."

Holy shit.

With that, I pulled her to me, my hands on her cute little ass. She threw her arms around my neck just as I'd hoped she would, and dropped her head back to give me access to her throat.

Her skin was velvety and warm, and I picked up a slight trace of cologne. My hands wandered from her behind to the long braid running down her back, which I wrapped around my fist like a rope.

With a quick yank, I spun her to face the window overlooking the lobby. As I did, she gasped and placed her hands against it for balance. Slipping my hands under her work tunic, I found her bra, which I pushed up to reach her nipples.

I rubbed the pads of my fingers over them at first, enough to kick off her arousal, and then took her little points between my thumbs and forefingers, rolling them until they were sharp peaks. When she ground her ass back against my growing cock, I suspected she might like it a little rough. So I pinched and pulled until, with a loud moan, her head fell forward and her breath grew raspy.

"How are you doing, baby?" I breathed in her ear, still working her tits.

"Mmmm," she murmured, "so good. So good."

I slipped my hand down the elastic waist of her pants to find her panties soaked through with goodness. I pressed through the silky fabric to feel the outline of her lips, and managed to burrow a finger between them, causing her to gasp again. Even though I was still outside, she ground down against my hand, begging for relief.

I stopped long enough to pull her top over her head, cast aside her bra, and yank her pants and panties down to her ankles. I helped her free one foot so I could widen her stance, and pulled her so she was bent from the waist into a ninety-degree angle, hands still pressed against the window for balance.

With my thumbs, I pulled her ass cheeks apart for a perfect view of her puckered rosebud and bare pussy lips, now delectably engorged and glistening with her fluids. I ran a finger between the cushiony flesh, and brought it up to my lips for a taste.

Amazing. Just like I knew it would be.

While I unbuckled my trousers, I whispered in her ear. "Fuck, you're hot, baby. And the way you taste makes me hard. Really hard."

She mumbled something.

"What's that darlin'?" I asked.

She straightened up and turned to face me. Completely naked, she took my goddamn breath away with her flawless, smooth skin, and slight curves.

"I asked, if I could suck you," she said quietly, her eyes heavy-lidded.

Well, shit.

I gathered our clothes and made a little pillow for her knees. Without hesitation, she dropped, looking up at me so earnestly I almost asked her to marry me right there. I held my dick out for her, and with our gazes locked, she ran her lips over my head just to the sensitive ridge, and tongued my precum.

Holy fucking shit. Thank god I was next to the window so I had something to lean on.

I watched my beauty from above, her little tits jiggling with the movement of her head. I wove my fingers into her plaited hair, and held her as she pistoned me.

I knew I wasn't going to last long, which was fine really, because I was certain I'd have the energy in due time to properly fuck her brains out. But for now, we were in a public place, and time was wasting.

Opening her mouth wide, she slowly engulfed me until my entire cock had disappeared down her throat. She somehow held it there for a moment, incredibly without gagging, and then began to piston her head up and down. I wanted my dick in her pussy or ass, but for now her mouth was more than fine.

Mustn't be a greedy bastard.

To meet her movements, I thrust my hips in her face and she took me deeper yet, her half-shut eyes watering, saliva running down her chin. She was entirely spaced out, grunting and breathing hard. Her only instinct at that moment was to please me, which was driving me out of my fucking mind.

My balls pulled in tight, until they ached, and I knew my release was imminent. "I'm getting close, baby. So close…"

I became a coiled ball of tension, and there was no holding back. "I'm coming, I'm going to fill your mouth right NOW."

I groaned loudly enough to be heard down the hall, and I didn't give a fuck as my load started pumping my load down Roxy's throat. Her eyes widened with surprise as she took my cum like a champ. Convulsing rapidly, I spurted for what felt like an eternity, and when I was finally done, Roxy pulled back and looked up at me with a beatific smile, one little drip running down her chin.

If only I could have taken a photo. No, fuck that, I didn't need a photo. I'd never forget what she looked like at that moment. It was the most amazing thing I'd ever seen.

13

ROXY VANDENBERG

I STROLLED ACROSS CAMPUS, lost in thought. I had plenty of time before my next class and was thinking through my conversation with Silas of the day before… and other things.

"Why are you still working at the hotel?" he'd asked me over lunch at a little bistro not far from the movie theater he was working on.

After we'd had our sexy encounter in the hotel storage room.

Which I was still tingling from.

I nibbled my Reuben sandwich. "I guess I'm not ready to quit just yet. Still thinking about the offer from you guys."

He adjusted his glasses and looked at me, making me wish I could read his mind. Did he really want me? Did any of them? Or were they just feeling sorry for me?

And had they done this before?

"I understand," he said, "I know it's a lot to take in. I don't know why it surprised me that you were still working at the hotel. It's true, you haven't given us a definitive answer yet, so why would you have quit."

"I just need a little… time."

I actually needed more than time. I needed to get my shit together. I was freaking terrified.

After the guys had spelled out how they wanted to help me—incredibly generous by any measure—I'd immediately run to Birdie and Jessa because they were the only people I could share something like this with. They each had their own—what I liked to call—'professor harem.' And they were pretty freaking happy. Ecstatic, even. It's like they were poster-children for student/professor naughtiness.

Which had always struck me as hot as hell. I'd just never thought I'd be living it. Or thinking about living it.

Birdie had connected with her guys after she ill-advisedly—Jessa and I being the ill advisors—had written an English essay about how she was a virgin. One thing led to another after she tried frantically to get the essay back before anyone read it. It was too late, and as her teachers got to know her better, they fell head over heels for her.

It wasn't hard to understand. She was pretty, wicked smart, and loved literature at least as much as the guys did. An English teacher's wet dream come true, if you asked me.

Jessa, on the other hand, had bewitched her men

with her artistic talent and off-beat ways. A beautiful bohemian, she left behind college boys and found her happy with older men, also instructors at Wellshire. Her new loves were smitten with her, and knew just how lucky they were.

But me? Well, to begin with, I didn't have a hell of a lot to offer. I was an average student with no plans to change the world. My family was broke, my dad a potential criminal, and my only means of making money was cleaning hotel rooms. I supposed I was averagely pretty, but the Wellshire campus was full of girls far more attractive than me.

Not exactly a prize catch.

That's why I was so hesitant to comfortably consider the guys' offer. What was in it for them?

Sex?

Maybe, but they could get that anywhere. They were gorgeous, smart, and successful.

My head was spinning.

"You know, Rox, you are so full of shit," Jessa said when I'd sat down with both her and Birdie to discuss my predicament.

"That's nice, Jess. I ask you for help and you tell me I'm full of shit."

Shaking her head, she reached for my hand. "You know what I mean, Rox! You are amazing. Look at yourself. You're gorgeous, sexy, and fun. What guy wouldn't want to be with you?"

Hmmm. I don't know. Maybe the last couple guys who'd dumped me?

Birdie sat back on her bed, back propped against the wall. "You know my position on this. I've never been happier. Being with professors is fucking hot." She leaned forward and lowered her voice as if she were sharing a secret. "You know what really gets me revved up about the guys? How all the other students on campus stare at them, flirt with them, and try to snag their attention. But they come home to me at the end of the day, and every day I make them happy they did."

Then it occurred to me, why Paloma might be all over my ass about Arrow.

She liked him. And she could't believe he might prefer me over her. It would be fun to bring this up next time we ran into each other.

"Do you get tired of… you know, all the sex?" I asked.

She and Jessa looked at each other and burst out laughing.

"Are you fucking kidding? Have you seen Cary, Kai, and Leo? You think you would ever get tired of them? They're my dream come true. Endless sex with three beautiful men who I also happen to have fallen for," she said.

And there we had it. My situation was completely different from Birdie's and Jessa's. While unconventional, they were in relationships—real relationships— with men they loved.

That's not what Baird's, Arrow's, or Silas's offer was about.

Or was it?

"You guys, I love that they want to help me. But they aren't like *into* me. It's kind of a… sugar daddy arrangement or something."

Jessa rolled her eyes and flopped back on her own bed. "Oh. My. God," she whined. Then she popped back up to sitting. "You think they'd make you an offer like this if they were just so-so about you?"

She had a point.

I just wasn't sure how I felt about them. And that was at least as important as how they felt about me.

Right?

"Oh. Look who it is."

I turned to find Paloma had sidled up next to me on my way to class. I started walking faster, but of course, she matched my pace.

She was like a bad penny. I couldn't get rid of her.

So I stopped. Right in the middle of the crowded sidewalk, busy as rush hour with students hustling to and from their commitments. People streamed around us as we blocked their path, jostling us and occasionally throwing us side-eye for holding them up.

But I didn't care.

I got right in her face. "What do you want?" I hissed.

She wore her hair long and straight, parted down the middle like nearly all the girls on campus. She was very pretty, but the upper half of her face was immobile, making it difficult to read her expression, and her top lip resembled a duck bill with the unnatural way it protruded.

Why someone our age loaded up on fillers and Botox like she did was beyond me.

She smiled, her duck lip straining the skin stretched over it. "Just wanted to say hi to the *townie whore*."

Really?

I gnashed my teeth until it hurt, my entire body tensing. What this bitch didn't realize was that the more she pissed me off, the more likely she was going to get a hard, painful slap across her face. Or worse.

I could control myself. To a point.

"Paloma. Don't you have anything better to do?" I asked in an overly sweet, mocking tone. "Isn't there some frat boy you could be fucking? Or test you could be failing? You know, all the things you're so good at? Or is this what you're best at, being a total fucking cunty bitch?"

She froze for a moment, her mouth dropping open, then got her mojo back as if she were just warming up. "I just wanted to let you know that before you spread your legs, *I* was making inroads with Professor Menken. *We* were going to date."

And there we had it. It was just as I'd thought. Paloma had spilled exactly what I'd been thinking, which explained *everything*. She had the hots for Arrow. Why had it taken me that long to figure it out?

There was so much I wanted to say.

"Look, Paloma. To begin with, I did not 'spread my legs' for anyone. And I certainly didn't cockblock you from Menken. I don't know what sort of inroads you thought you were making, but did it ever occur to you that you might have been mistaken? That he would want nothing to do with a phony-ass basic bitch like you?"

"You're wrong," she said, hesitantly.

"Fine. I don't own him. Go for it."

And give us all a good laugh.

She looked me up and down and with a huff, turned and walked off.

The problem was, we were both heading for Arrow's class, so I had to watch the back of her head until we got there.

And when we did, I sat clear across the room from her. She took a front-row seat that day, crossing and uncrossing her legs for the benefit of Arrow's glance.

I wanted to laugh out loud at her, but Arrow was returning our latest exams, face-down on our desks.

He glanced at me briefly when he laid mine on my desk, and a delicious little flutter bounced around in my stomach.

I hadn't studied much for Arrow's finance test. I'd just been so distracted by everything going on, not to mention busy with work and other… things.

But I wasn't expecting the C- I got when I flipped my test over.

Fuck.

The night before the exam, when I should have

been studying my ass off, I'd taken an extra cleaning shift at the hotel.

It was an impossible balance. I needed to work more to pay bills, but the work cut into my study time.

Normally, a lousy grade wouldn't faze me. After all, I got them frequently. But this one was different.

It was from Arrow. And I was embarrassed.

As he dove into his lecture, I could swear he was avoiding my gaze. Which was just as well, because after our night together, I was pretty sure to dissolve into a gooey mess every time his piercing blue eyes met mine.

But he wasn't avoiding me because we were turning each other on. He was avoiding me because I'd gotten a shitty grade in his class. I'd disappointed him.

As I was fidgeting in my seat, wishing a hole would open in the ground for me to disappear into, my phone vibrated.

The phone the guys had just turned on for me.

It was a text from my mother.

Honey, can you call me?

I tucked the phone back in my pocket, planning to call her as soon as class was over.

But it vibrated again.

It's important, Roxy. I need to talk to you.

So I grabbed my things and quietly left class, Arrow's gaze burning into my backside as I did.

"Mom? What's up?"

I wasn't in the mood for conversation. After all, since the day my parents' house had been invaded by government officials or whomever they were, I hadn't heard from them to see how I was doing or where I was staying.

"Honey, it's bad," she said in a shaky voice.

No shit.

"Dad's... there's a warrant out for your father's arrest," she said with a sob.

Jesus. Was she really that surprised?

"C'mon, Mom. You didn't see that coming?" I asked.

She held the phone away to spare me her wailing. "How can you be so callous?"

Um, maybe because I recently found out I was neither enrolled in college, nor had a place to live?

That will harden a girl up, real fast.

"Where is he right now?"

"On the run," she wept.

On the run? What was this? *The Fugitive?*

I turned to see Arrow's class emptying into the corridor. I didn't want to talk to him, at least not yet, so I darted down the closest staircase and outside the business building.

This was bad. My mother had been right. But it wasn't just bad for my family or me. It could also be bad for the guys. It could reflect poorly on them, or follow them in their endeavors if it was known they were associated with me.

I couldn't do that to them.

I needed to find my father and convince him to turn himself in.

That would be a step in the right direction.

14

BAIRD PRIESTLY

"WHY'RE you so quiet today, Roxy? You sleep all right?"

We were only in day two of Roxy's 'trial period.' She'd suggested we try out our arrangement for a week or so to see how it went.

It was a great idea. I was sorry I hadn't thought of it.

So, on her first real night with us, she made a sandwich and went up to the guest room—now her room—and closed the door.

Which was fine. God knew I liked my time to myself, and living with other people sometimes necessitated disappearing into one's room. I had a Boys Club meeting to attend, anyway.

When she emerged to head over to campus the next morning, her manner was much the same as it had been the night before.

Did she already hate the house? Was she regretting her 'trial period?'

Regardless, she was in some sort of crisis, and I

didn't like that. At all. No matter where our relationship went, I didn't want to see her suffer. Ever.

I told the guys that, since she was working for me a couple hours before her classes, I'd try to find out what I could. Arrow mentioned she'd gotten a poor grade in his class, and that might have been bothering her on top of everything else. When they'd discussed it, she got very upset even though he offered to do all he could to help her with the course material.

She was embarrassed. I got it. We all did.

So in addition to her poor grade in Arrow's class, she had a lot of other shit going on, too. Hell, if I were her I didn't know how I'd even get out of bed in the morning. I wanted her to believe things were looking up. But it was the kind of thing that, if you didn't see it yourself, it served no purpose for someone to point it out to you.

She had to find her own way out of her funk. We were helping all we could, god knew, but she had to see the light at the end of the tunnel herself.

And this morning, as she bent over a rickety, university-issue filing cabinet in my office, she painstakingly worked through the huge pile of paperwork I'd been neglecting for weeks, organizing and getting it all out of my sight.

It seemed sort of quaint to hang on to paper copies of things in the digital age, but keeping certain stuff was one of the university's quirks. Those of us who advised students groused about the requirement to no end, creating sky-high piles until they could no longer be ignored.

Or, we were lucky enough to meet a student like Roxy who needed a job.

So to speak.

I hated to see our girl sad. I mean, shit, I shouldn't even be calling her 'our girl,' but I—and I think Arrow and Silas—were committed to helping her out in any way we could. And looking at her now, bent over my filing cabinet with her long blonde hair hiding her face, I could swear I heard a couple surreptitious sniffles.

Having her in such close proximity while I was trying to work was a challenge. Her occasional sighs, and the scent of her shampoo filled the room, just like thoughts of the fun we'd had together filled my mind. I wouldn't have minded locking my door and bending her right over...

But I wouldn't do that. She was turning inward at the moment, and I could respect that. I trusted that she'd tell me what was going on when she was ready. But I also wanted to remind her I was here for her.

In more than just the obvious ways.

In answer to my question, she kept her head down, but cleared her throat. "I slept fine last night. You?"

"I slept great. I always do. But it looks like there's something going on for you."

She finally looked my way, and it was no surprise that her eyes were bloodshot, and the tip of her nose pink.

"Hey, grab a seat on this stool here. You need a break."

She smiled wanly. "I'm okay. Just got a lot on my mind." She slammed a filing cabinet drawer shut so hard, a cloud of dust rose off the floor surrounding it.

I looked at her without saying anything. I was here for her without pressuring her to spill her guts. It was part of my training as an academic advisor. Listening was at least as important as speaking. And sometimes silence said it all.

She sighed deeply, her shoulders slumping. "There… there's been a new development." She took a seat and crossing her legs, tapped her Converse Chuck sneaker on the floor, looking off into the distance, as if a solution might appear out of thin air.

"I could tell something was up. Anything I can do to help?"

I could think of a few ways to take her mind off her troubles.

Down boy.

She finally met my gaze. "My dad is wanted by the authorities. Like the kind of authorities that arrest your ass."

She started wringing her hands.

"Holy shit."

She nodded. "According to my mom, he's on the run." She gave a weak laugh. "*On the run*. So dramatic. So cops and robbers."

"Do you know what he did?"

She looked up at me, her eyes haunted and her chin trembling.

"He stole money from the construction company where he worked. And I guess he wasn't paying the mortgage on the house because that's gone now, too."

Jesus. This guy fucked up six ways from Sunday. And the collateral damage he left in his wake, like Roxy, was massive. Must be a hell of a guy.

"I'm so ashamed of him," she said, a teardrop falling on her clenched fists. "It's humiliating for the whole family."

I reached for her hands, small and cold in mine. "You need to understand one thing right away, Roxy. Your dad's actions are no reflection on you. No one blames you. You aren't the one who stole from the company. You aren't the one who stopped payments on the house. You are, however, impacted by his actions, and that's unfair. Very unfair."

She gripped my fingers back as if she'd gotten strength from unburdening herself, and just when I thought I needed to let her get back to her filing, I stood and pulled her to me, instead. I wanted to make her pain go away.

Just like I'd gotten away from the pain of my own past, I wanted to take her someplace safe, as well.

I knew only one real way to do that.

With my finger under her chin, I tilted her pretty face up to mine and began to devour her lips, so soft under mine. Our tongues explored each other's and after a moment, she began to relax in my arms.

I could take her away, if only for a moment.

I pulled the elastic from her ponytail with one hand, and raked my fingers through her lush hair. She sighed from the sensation, and pressed herself more tightly to me.

"There… there's more to the story. At least I think there is," she said.

I pulled back to look at her. "What is it?"

She bit her lip, then nodded. "It might affect you."

"What? How?"

"My… my dad was a subcontractor for the firm you hired to renovate the movie theater. I'm afraid whatever he's done might have messed up your project."

Well, shit. For a moment I felt like someone had hit me, but I took a deep breath. I could handle this.

"You're right, this is not good news. But we don't even know if it's true. If it is, we'll deal with it. We'll figure it out. But I repeat, you are not to blame for this. And I'm glad you told me."

"I am too," she said, letting me take her trembling hands. "Thank you, Baird," she added quietly, in between kisses.

"You're welcome, Roxy."

I locked my office door and turned to find her smiling. She sank back onto the stool where she'd been sitting and pulled me closer. I stood in front of her, my crotch perfectly level to her mouth.

Nice.

While she undid my blue jeans, I reached for her tits, which, to my happy surprise, were free of a bra. I kneaded her through her denim blouse, and started working her buttons.

But I had trouble standing a moment later when she took the entirety of me into her mouth, all the way to the root of my rock-hard cock.

"Holy fuck," I groaned, my head dropping back as I grasped hers for balance. "Baby, your tongue…"

She moaned lightly, releasing me to my sensitive ridge, and lashed her tongue around and across my head. "So good," she murmured.

Fucking right.

I didn't want to explode in her mouth, which I was moments away from doing, but before I pushed her off my cock, I gripped her head harder and bucked my hips, pistoning in and out of her mouth until I banged against the back of her throat.

"Oh god," I said, pulling out, leaving her with an open mouth and watering eyes. "I'm going to fuck you now, darlin'."

I shed my jeans and pulled her to her feet. Before I could even get to hers, she had them down around her ankles and had freed one foot from the tangle of fabric. She propped her ass onto the edge of my desk, and leaning back on her elbows, spread her legs for me.

If it had been hard to hold my cum when she was blowing me, she was killing me now, showing off her shaved, pink pussy, her lips puffy with her slit barely hiding the place where I was about to bury my cock.

I sheathed myself with a condom from my pants

pocket and lifted her legs onto my shoulders, pulling her ass off the desk for perfect positioning.

"Are you good, baby?"

She gave me a coy smile, "I am, Baird."

She reached under her legs and grabbed my cock, pointing it up toward her hungry opening. As soon as I was notched there, I pushed about halfway in.

She gasped as her head fell back, and then released a laugh that I wanted to hear over and over again.

"Are you ready for my dick, baby? Are you ready for the whole thing?" I asked.

Her head still lolling, she managed to groan as her only response. She was fucking amazing. Tight, wet, and greedy for me.

So I drove all the way into her, burying my cock as deep as it had just been in her mouth. She squealed when I bottomed out inside her, but only grabbed my forearms and pulled me deeper.

"God Baird, your cock…"

But she couldn't finish and instead just dug her nails into my back. My slow strokes already had her pulsing around my dick, her first orgasm only moments away.

I knew I wasn't going to last long, and I wanted to see my beauty explode with pleasure before I did. I gripped her ass tightly with one hand as I continued to pound her pussy, bringing my forefinger to my mouth to wet it. I quickly reached back down and eased my finger into her tight ass, catching her by surprise. She immediately yielded to the pressure. I never would have dreamed that our girl was into ass play, but thank god she was because we guys loved it as much as we loved to breathe.

Her moans turned almost to growls, her breath coming in raspy bursts, and she began to shudder under me, throwing her head back and forth, her eyes half-open and unfocused.

This was when I let loose on her. I pumped that pussy like it was the last one I'd ever have, burying my finger all the way up her ass. Her shriek set me off. My balls tightened and my load erupted as I pummeled her until I had nothing left.

Afterward, I scooped her onto my lap where her head fell on my shoulder. We gripped each other tightly, and I hoped she was that much closer to calling an end to her 'trial period,' and diving into what the guys and I were really offering her.

15

ROXY VANDENBERG

"IT'S JUST STUNNING."

With one hand holding a too-big construction hat on my head, I did a complete three-sixty-degree turn to take in the resurrection of the movie theater that had been such an important part of my childhood.

I walked over to the grand staircase, which Silas's team thankfully hadn't done away with in the new design. Stepping over construction debris, I touched the carved wooden handrail that curved up and to the second floor, out of sight. For as long as I could remember, I was enchanted by this display of grandeur, always amazed I could experience it for the price of a cheap movie ticket.

"The apartments will be upstairs, right?" I asked, looking up to where the new third floor, which was, at the moment, not much more than wooden studs, open to the sky above.

This was a massive freaking project. I couldn't

believe I was even allowed inside to take a look. But I guess if you knew the head architect, you were golden.

I'd been in several construction sites in my life, having been sneaked into them by my father, after hours when no one else was around. Looking back, he might have had access as a subcontractor, although he really had no business snooping around them, much less bringing his kids to see them. I guess that entitled behavior was par for the course.

I'd never seen anything quite like this movie theater renovation, though, which kept a grip on the old beauty of the interior, while building it out for a new use. I looked up again at the exposed sky and thought about how the project was still so raw. It had a long way to go. And Silas couldn't stop smiling about it.

My stomach churned with the knowledge I was about to share with him.

He pointed to where the snack concessions used to be, where I had bought countless boxes of Milk Duds as a kid. "We could do one or two apartments here on the ground floor too, but it's looking like the Boys Club wants to keep these spaces for offices and meeting rooms. Once we start meeting here, we won't be using the hotel for our meetings anymore."

I know he didn't want me spending as much time at the hotel, either, but one step at a time.

I still hadn't decided what to do about the guys' offer. Thanks to a big pep talk, as well as some mind-blowing sexy time, Baird had essentially dragged me out of the funk I'd been in the day before. But my problems weren't gone. Not by a long shot.

Although I was feeling positive about the opportunities before me, and for the first time in a long time believed I might be able to rise above the mess my father had created for the family, there was one last hurdle that could throw a wrench in everybody's plans.

Both literally and figuratively.

And that hurdle was coming like a freight train.

But before it did, I let myself enjoy both Silas's tour and his company. If it were the last time I got to spend with him up close and alone, I wanted to clearly remember the imperfect perfection that was his face.

His heavy hipster glasses drew attention away from his slightly crooked nose, the result of a childhood bike wreck, he'd told me. If you asked me about it, it made him a thousand times more handsome.

It was like when people said they liked the gap between my teeth. I hated it, but it was unique. No doubt about that.

And Silas always smelled good. So damn good.

All that, mixed with the memory of messing around with him in the hotel mezzanine, was enough to leave me tongue-tied.

So I tried not to stare at him for too long at a stretch as he showed me around the theater. I didn't want him to know what a dork I was.

Although the chances of his seriously thinking I was some sort of 'cool girl,' like my friend Jessa, were pretty slim. I just didn't have the game for that.

Yeah, wasn't fooling anyone.

Which brought me back to the question of *why me?*

Cripes, the amount of time I'd spent wondering that. But I guess that plagued anyone suddenly experiencing a stroke of good luck, especially after a shitty run like the one I'd had. And was still having, depending on whom you asked.

Couldn't get ahead of myself yet.

"Shall we take a look upstairs?" he suggested. "Be careful, though. Parts of the place are still pretty rough."

When we got to the second floor, I could see exactly what he was talking about. Framing for the apartments was well underway. But on that particular day, no one was working.

I thought I might know why.

"Where is everyone?" I asked cautiously.

"Not sure. Our contractor called to let us know they were waiting for some supplies. So, the crew is at another job today."

That's what they'd told him?

I wondered if I should tell him the truth. The disgraceful, ugly truth.

Which was that my father had embezzled so much from the construction firm, that until their cash-flow problems were resolved, this project was on hold.

I was pretty sure the firm hadn't been truthful when they blamed the hold-up on supplies. Which was not a good way to go, because the truth was going to come out sooner rather than later.

So, Dad had not only fucked up my life but also that of those involved in the renovation of this old theater.

Not to mention the happy families that were slated to move in when it was complete.

It was amazing how one person could cause so much destruction.

"Yeah, we should actually be farther along," Silas added. "But with construction, things always get off track. We should still be able to open on our projected date."

His enthusiasm for the project was breaking my heart. What if it was never finished? What if Dad had stolen all their money?

Which he pretty much had.

Yup, my father had basically stolen from the Boys Club.

And Silas didn't know it yet.

"Hey, Silas, can you sit down for a moment?" I asked, pointing at two paint-splattered folding chairs.

He took a seat, continuing to look at the place with wonder. "You know, this is the kind of project I'd always dreamed about. Taking something old and grand, and repurposing it."

Ugh.

"In fact," he continued, "I have something to share with you. Something confidential."

I guess my news would have to wait a moment.

"I… have been offered a position with an architectural firm. Actually, the one I worked for before I came to Wellshire."

From the expression on his face, I wasn't sure whether this was great news, or just so-so news. He wasn't giving anything away. Perhaps because he wasn't sure how he felt.

I could relate.

"Wow. Congratulations."

He looked off in the distance, nodding slightly.

"You have a big decision to make, huh? I guess when you've become a professor, you don't want to just walk away. Is that what's holding you back?"

He took a deep breath. "That's part of it. The reason I left to begin with was the crazy long hours, and I wasn't really doing work I was excited about. But they've come back to me with a management position, and I'd be heading up their retail practice. I'd get to design stores."

"Wow. But it sounds like it would be long hours again, just like it was before. I mean, if you're the boss, you have more work to do than anyone, right?"

God, I felt like shit, chit-chatting with him, when I was about to drop a bomb.

He laughed. "Yeah. I'd be back to the horrendous hours. But it sounds like it would be more interesting. And, I'd get paid a hell of a lot more. There is one downside, though."

He turned to me.

"What? What's the downside?" I asked.

He rolled his shoulders like he was tense. "I'd... have to move. Leave town. In fact, move clear across the country."

Oh.

My stomach churned and I kicked a scrap of wood on the floor by my foot.

For some naïve reason, I'd assumed the job was local. How silly was that?

And now the churning in my stomach was moving up toward my throat. I leaned forward to disguise the discomfort, and played it off like I was tying my shoe.

"Oh," I said. "That's interesting. You might leave town."

My throat was suddenly dry, and I wanted to get out of there really, really badly. What the hell? I hadn't even told the guys whether or not I wanted to be with them, but I was getting all butt-hurt that Silas was considering leaving town.

What a hypocrite I was.

But I had something I had to say before I started worrying about my own problems again.

And once I did, I had a feeling Silas's opportunity to leave town wouldn't be having any impact on my life, anyway.

Because the guys would surely kick me to the curb as a result.

"Hey, Silas, there's something I want to tell you. There's some new… information about my dad. At first I thought it only affected me and my family. But I've since learned it actually impacts you. And Baird and Arrow."

He frowned. "What? What happened?"

I took in his good looks like I was having my last

glass of water ever. I wanted to savor his crooked nose and everything else about him.

"I…"

Fuck. Just spill it.

"Silas, I found out my dad was embezzling from the company where he worked, which was subcontractor to the firm you hired to do this renovation. He took all the money paid to his company and… well, I don't know how long it will take the main construction company to recover." I gave a weak laugh even though it was anything but funny.

Silas's face went blank as he put two-and-two together.

"Are you telling me…" He trailed off.

I didn't blame him.

I looked down. I couldn't face him. The shame was too overwhelming. "His actions have slowed down if not stopped this movie theater project along with several others the company has in the works."

His head tweaked the tiniest bit. "Where is your dad now?"

Of course he was going to ask this. "I… don't know. No one knows, according to my mother. There is an arrest warrant out for him, and he's on the run."

I couldn't have made up a crazier story if I'd tried.

"Damn."

"I'm so, so sorry, Silas."

My dad's bad juju was like the gift that kept on giving. Seriously. How else could the man possibly fuck me up, and everyone else in his wake?

I had an urge to run. Just run away from the shit-show that was my life. Start over where I knew no one. Start over where my shit couldn't follow me.

Was that even possible?

"I just cannot believe him. I'm so ashamed. My whole family is. And now his actions are impacting you and the guys." I dropped my head into my hands.

That's when I felt Silas's hand on my shoulder. My head snapped up, and saw him peering down at me, wearing a small smile.

It was a kind smile. The sort that left me with a lump in my throat.

"I'm sorry—" I started to say, as if I hadn't already said it enough times.

I had a feeling I'd never *stop* saying it.

Despite the look on his face, I was waiting for him to explode. No, actually, I wanted him to explode.

Tell me how pissed he was that my dad ruined everything. And then tell me to go home, collect my shit, and get the hell out.

Instead, he put his hands on my shoulders, and pulled me to my feet. He wrapped his arms around me in the kindest, sweetest gesture.

"Roxy, it's not your fault. You have nothing to do with all this." He stepped back to look directly at me. "It's a bummer, for sure. It's all kinds of fucked up. But we'll straighten it out. All is not lost."

It sure as hell felt like all was lost.

"I—"

But he cut me off by pressing his lips to mine.

When he pulled back, he took my hand to his lips, kissing that, too. "Roxy, I don't see it the way you do. You have to understand that. No one blames you. Not me, not Baird, and not Arrow. I know that's hard for you to accept. But please try to."

If they didn't blame me, maybe I shouldn't blame myself.

"Damn. That is quite a story, girl."

Jessa and I were huffing, crossing the campus with several of her paintings under each arm. Who knew a bunch of canvases could be so heavy?

And to make it even more of a cardio workout, she picked up the pace. "C'mon. I'm gonna be late."

We had a deadline for hanging Jessa's paintings in the campus art gallery. Of course, she waited until the last minute to decide which she wanted to display, and now we were rushing to meet the show curator.

"Is it that bad if you're late, Jess? I mean, can't Griff or Indy pull strings for you?"

Her head snapped in my direction, and I saw I'd asked the wrong question. But I didn't see what the big deal was. They were her boyfriends, and instructors in the art department. Wouldn't they want to help?

"I don't ask the guys for favors like that. It's not cool and besides, I want to make it on my own."

I respected that.

"Anyway, that is totally fucked, what your dad did, but obviously the guys are not blaming you. Where are you with accepting their offer?" she asked.

I still didn't know. I'd say that, over the course of a day, I'd decide to accept their offer, then decide to turn it down, at least a dozen times.

"I don't know, Jess. It's different for you. You fell in love. This feels like more of a sugar daddy arrangement. It's weird. I'm not sure it's for me."

We finally arrived at the gallery, where Jessa set down her paintings to pull open the front door.

"I think you're looking at it the wrong way," she said, gathering the paintings back into her arms and heading straight for a cart to set them on.

When her arms were free, she took mine, and then faced me straight on. "These men want to help you. Do you realize how fortunate you are? They can pretty much erase all your problems."

Okay fine. They might 'erase' all my problems, but then would I just have a new set to contend with?

16

ARROW MENKEN

"OH MY GOSH. Sorry I'm late."

I looked over my shoulder to find a red-faced and wild-haired Roxy come blowing into my office. In a blur, she dumped her backpack and coat on a corner chair, and set up her laptop on a flimsy little table I'd pulled out of storage.

"Don't worry about it, darlin'."

I hoped my voice wasn't tight. It wasn't that it was a problem for her to arrive late. She'd texted me that her last class went over time. What I was preoccupied with, but desperate to keep to myself, was the building tension around *will she or won't she?*

Yeah. I couldn't lie. Her self-imposed 'trial period' was killing me, and I was so enjoying having her around—for a variety of reasons—I found myself really hoping she'd stay.

Of course, it was completely her choice, and I'd

support whatever direction she wanted to go in. But I knew what I wanted. I knew what the guys wanted.

Shit, we'd discussed it late into the night when she was asleep.

It was cool we were all attracted to her. It made sense. We were good friends, and valued similar things. I never thought I might be sharing a woman with these guys, but after I'd gotten used to the idea, I'd realized it was hot as fuck.

Catching her breath, she turned to me from her makeshift work area. "Should I continue on the presentation for next week's class? Or do you need me to do something else?"

Something else…

Get a grip asshole.

"The presentation would be great. Thank you," I said, turning back to my own computer before I lost the battle to keep my thoughts clean and my hands to myself.

There she was, a regular college girl. But she was so much more than that. I loved her drive, and her ability, most of the time, to keep her chin up in the face of all that was raining down around her.

She was going to be fine. I knew she would. Things would turn a corner for her, one way or the other.

Despite my best intentions, I peeked at her anyway, watching her peck away at her keyboard, because I was such a goddamn smitten pussy. Her blonde hair nearly covered her pretty face, and her foot tapped with her overload of energy. She stopped what she was doing for a moment, and drew a finger to mouth, where she chewed on a nail. Then, in a new burst of energy, she got back to the keyboard, working like an artist struck by inspiration.

I had to say I was impressed. It was hard to get excited about making a presentation for a finance class. But Roxy was finding a way.

It was that 'light' that followed her, which attracted me like a moth to a flame.

I knew the other guys felt the same.

I was so fucked. *We* were so fucked.

She abruptly stopped, and turned to me, catching me staring. But she paid no attention. "Hey. Can I ask you a question, Arrow?"

"Sure Roxy."

Shit, it wasn't like I was getting any damn work done with her there. Her presence changed everything. Instead of my office smelling like the dusty hundred-year-old building it always did, it now carried the subdued scent of Roxy. Pure, clean Roxy

There was nothing better, I swear to god.

"Arrow, how is it you have such an amazing house? I know that's kind of a rude question, but you clearly don't live like the average professor. Not that I've been to any other professor's houses. It's just that growing up in a college town, you know these things."

I'd been waiting for her to ask that. She was no dummy. My house was a bit set back from the street for privacy, but it was certainly considered *lavish* by professor standards. When I first bought it, I wondered if I was making a mistake. Too showy or something. Didn't want to alienate my colleagues. God knew academics could be petty.

That was why I kept my circle of friends close. Baird and Silas knew my story, at least most of it. No one else needed to.

I took a deep breath. "I think you know I worked on Wall Street for several years before coming to Wellshire. When I was there I made… well, a good living. A very good living. That's how I was able to afford my nice house."

I wondered if I should also tell her that's how I was able to afford to give her a place to live and pay for her college. Sure, Baird and Silas were ready and willing to contribute, but since it had been my idea, and I had the cash, I wanted to pay for the bulk of it.

We'd see how comfortable they were with that. We were still in our 'trial period,' after all.

She turned to fully face me from her chair. "Well, that makes sense. Do you miss Wall Street? Silas was talking about his days at an architectural firm. You know, the ups and downs of that."

While I did occasionally toy with the idea of going back to Wall Street, I was pretty damn happy my time at Wellshire had brought Roxy into my life.

"Like anything, some things I miss, some things I don't. Being at the university is working well for me now. I'm still enjoying teaching. Who knows about a few years from now? Academia has its own ups and downs. So, has Silas told you about his opportunity?"

He had a conundrum for sure, and while he had a lot to think about, I suspect whether or not Roxy decided to stay in our lives would play a part in his decision.

She nodded and turned back to her laptop, moving charts around on her PowerPoint slides. "He did tell me. Sounds like a great opportunity."

"What do you think about his potentially leaving town?"

She halted, but only momentarily. Shit, she was good at giving nothing away when she didn't want to. "That would really be... something. Pulling up roots and... leaving."

Just then there was a loud rapping at my door, followed by its flying open.

Silas stuck his head inside. "Afternoon, friends," he said.

Shit, he looked happy.

"Hey. Speak of the devil. We were just talking about you and whether you're going to leave all this glamor behind," I said with a laugh, gesturing around my dumpy office.

He closed the door behind himself and pulled up an old cardboard box since there wasn't any place else to sit.

"I know, right? How could I leave all this?" he laughed.

"How's everything over at the movie theater, Silas?"

Roxy asked.

He took a deep breath. "Well, not much is happening right now. But that's to be expected."

A darkness washed over her face, and she turned back to her work.

I knew she felt like shit over what her father had done. I would too, if I were her. I just wish there were some way we could convince her we didn't blame her.

Silas looked at me knowingly and got to his feet. He approached Roxy from behind, and placed his hands on her shoulders.

Was he going with this where I thought he might be? As he gently rubbed her shoulders and neck, I turned around to press the lock on my office door.

"Hey," he said to her in a low voice. "This has nothing to do with you. If I've said it once, I've said it a thousand times" He bent closer and, pushing her hair out of the way, ran his lips up the shell of her ear.

From where I sat, I watched her hands fall off the keyboard into her lap, and her neck arch to give him better access.

Fuck, the way she was so responsive just about killed me.

His lips wandered from her ear, down her neck, and around to her mouth. He pulled her to her feet to face him.

With one hand holding her head as he kissed her, his other brushed over a breast, then down her stomach, and landed below the zipper of her blue jeans.

Even with the thick fabric there, his hand between her legs elicited a long sigh as she tightened her grip on his arms.

Silas looked at me. "She's gorgeous, isn't she, Arrow?"

She sure as hell was. And watching her get turned on brought my dick to an instant erection.

"She's amazing. Just amazing," I said, clearing a spot on my desk.

While Silas kissed and felt her through her jeans, I approached her from behind. Lifting her hair, I brushed my lips over her warm, soft neck, inhaling her scent, and lightly pressing my erection against her ass.

"You good, baby?" I whispered.

"Oh yes," she murmured with a nod.

"Okay. Then how about we have you come over to my desk?" I asked.

Silas stepped aside, and I took Roxy's hand.

"I want you naked. Is that okay, beautiful?" I asked.

She met my gaze and with a coy smile, nodded.

I pulled her hoodie off and reached behind her to get rid of her bra, her perky tits bouncing into view.

I could hear Silas behind me, breathing.

Then I bent to remove her shoes and socks, and when those were out of the way, I opened the jeans Silas had been massaging her through, and lowered them and her panties to her ankles. She stepped out of them and was naked. Completely naked.

She leaned back on the desk with her hands, her

smooth skin and slim figure captivating me completely. I wanted to taste her from head to toe. I hardly knew where to start.

"Spread your legs, pretty girl," Silas growled, propping her ass up on the desk and putting a hand on her knees to coax them open.

And what a view we had when she did. Her smooth, shaved pussy was perfection, her lips puffy with need and her juices flowing. I was dying to plunge my tongue into the small slit of her opening, and maybe her ass too.

But, for now, Silas had beaten me to the punch.

He kneeled before her, where she sat on the desk, and gently pried her open with his thumbs. With a perfect view of her clit, he zeroed in on that, surrounding it with his lips.

She moaned at the contact, her head dropping back, her hips pushing into his face.

I took the opportunity to kiss her while I pulled out my cock. As soon as she realized that I had, she took me in hand, slowly stroking me, her thumb rubbing precum around the head of my dick, nearly causing an immediate explosion in her hand.

I pushed everything off my desk to make room for her to lie back, and when she did, I walked around to the side of the desk her head was hanging off. Positioning myself against her lips, I pushed inside her mouth.

"Fuck Silas. She feels good, doesn't she," I rasped, playing with her tits.

He emerged from between her legs and pulled a condom out of his pants pocket. He sheathed himself, then poised at her opening.

"Roxy, baby, are you gonna let me fuck your sweet pussy?" he asked.

"Mmmm hmmm," she said, her mouth full of my dick.

He hooked his arms under her legs, raising her ass off the desk, and plunged inside.

"Jesus, she's tight, Arrow," he grunted, his eyes squeezed shut.

I had a feeling he was going to last about as long as I was. Which was not long at all.

In fact, Roxy reached for my balls and as soon as they were in her warm hand, my eruption started. "Oh fuck, I'm coming, baby. I'm coming in your mouth," I shouted, glad that no one else on my floor had office hours that day.

Because we were putting on a hell of a show.

She swallowed what she could, occasionally sputtering and coughing, and when I pulled out, I wiped her face with the tail of my shirt. With Silas pummeling her at the edge of the desk, she propped herself up on her elbows, and started to quiver.

"Oh, oh, god, I'm coming *now*," she mumbled, bucking against Silas's long drives.

"I can feel your pussy grabbing me, oh god yeah, baby," he groaned, shoving his cock in her one more time.

As he shook, he held her legs, his face screwed up almost as if it were in pain, gasping for breath.

She, in turn, fell back on my desk, her eyes closed, trying to catch her own breath.

When Silas opened his eyes and glanced my way, and I knew we were thinking the same thing.

17

ROXY VANDENBERG

"Oh my god. Dad. What are you doing here?"

My father looked happy to see me. I couldn't say I felt the same about him.

But what could I do? He was my dad.

I gave him a quick once-over to see if he looked any different. For some reason I expected him to, with everything that had recently come to light.

But he looked like the same old construction manager dad he always had, with his plaid flannel shirt, well-worn blue jeans, steel toed boots, and rough, callused hands that had fascinated me as a kid.

Still, I sensed something different about him, which I was pretty sure boiled down to how I felt about the man. I didn't hate him. I couldn't. But at the moment, I sure didn't feel very fond of him.

"Roxy, thank god. I was hoping I would find you here," he said, furtively looking around the hotel lobby.

I didn't blame him for being nervous. After all, he was a wanted man.

"Dad, you shouldn't be here," I hissed, motioning for him to follow me toward a quiet corner.

It was my last day working as a maid. I wasn't one hundred percent committed to a long-term thing with the guys, but if I were going to do odd jobs for all three of them, there was no time to work at the hotel. I'd miss my friend Lolo. But our manager? Barney could take a hike.

So, Dad was very lucky he'd caught me on my way out, because if he'd looked for me tomorrow, they'd have told him I was no longer employed there.

"Roxy, I need your help. I've been staying here at the hotel," he said.

What? How?

"Are you kidding?" I asked.

"Yeah. Been staying in my room. Just coming out late at night to get fast food and groceries. I was pretty sure the authorities wouldn't think of looking for me here."

He was right. My dad at an expensive hotel? Not likely.

All my issues of the past weeks began to bubble to the surface, where I'd been trying to keep them under wraps. But I gulped down the fury rising in my chest. Now was not the time to tell my dad what I thought of the shit he was dragging the family through.

"Dad, *how* are you paying to stay here?" I asked, afraid of the answer I was going to get.

"Credit card, Rox. But it's a bad credit card. They don't know yet. I'm eventually going to get kicked out."

Holy shit. How did my father go from being a normal guy with two kids, a wife, and a house in the suburbs, to being a major fucking grifter?

Or had he been like this all along, and we just never knew?

The shit was just getting deeper.

"Dad, do you know what you've done here? You left me with no place to live and no way to stay in school. A heads up would have been nice if you didn't have the money to pay for your part of my tuition, don't you think?"

He hung his head. "I know, Rox. I messed up big time. I got into a hole and I kept thinking I could get out until it all collapsed on my head. I've lost everything," he said, his voice breaking.

"Yes, Dad, you have. And you're only making it worse by trying to hide."

He looked up at me, panic widening his eyes. "I can't go to jail, Roxy. If I do, I can never make things right."

"Dad, that's the first step to making things right. You can't run away from this. You've got to come to your senses. Turn yourself in."

"I... I... I..." he started to say.

But our attention was directed elsewhere.

"Oh hey, baby," Baird called, walking toward me with Arrow and Silas right behind.

I froze. I couldn't move or speak, and I wasn't sure I

was even breathing. I could hear, however, and as the guys approached, my dad's face switched from fear about his situation, to confusion.

"Look who it is," Baird said, reaching me first and planting a huge kiss on my lips.

Then he turned to my father. "Hi there," he said, extending his hand, "I'm Baird Priestly. Do you work here at the hotel, too?" he asked with a polite smile, making assumptions about Dad's working man garb.

Before either Dad or I could find our words, Arrow and Silas caught up, both greeting me with enthusiastic kisses, and a couple nice squeezes to my ass.

All. In. Front. Of. Dad.

Yup.

He cleared his throat, momentarily distracted from his criminality, and looked from one guy to the other before settling on Baird.

"No, young man, I do not *work* here at the hotel. I am a *guest* here. And I am also Roxy's father."

Baird's eyebrows shot up and he looked at the other guys. "Well. This is a surprise," he said cautiously.

Dad turned toward me. "Roxy, why did three men just kiss you?"

Oh, *now* he wants to act like a father?

"Um, Dad—" I started to say.

But he cut me off. "I don't know what you three think you're doing, kissing my daughter like that, but that is not acceptable—"

I tried to cut him off. "Dad, wait—"

But this time Silas cut me off. "Mr. Vandenberg, we

are... Roxy's friends. We just came to pick her up for a celebratory dinner. She's leaving her job here at the hotel."

Okay, Silas, didn't need to tell Dad all that...

"What? You've quit your job here?" he asked.

"Yeah, Dad. Arrow, Silas, and Baird here have offered me work. It will, um, pay better than my maid job. Which is important since, you know, you are no longer able to help with tuition."

Dad frowned. Where did this man get his nerve?

"Oh, and what kind of work is that? I saw one of them squeeze your ass."

I shrugged. I had to get out of here. I couldn't help my father. I also couldn't explain to him what I was doing with the guys. He wouldn't get it.

I put my hand on Dad's arm. "Look, Dad. We're leaving now. I don't want to get involved in whatever fugitive game you're playing. So, good luck with everything."

Baird took my hand and the four of us started to walk away.

"Okay," Dad called after me. "I see what's going on here. You... you deserve to be in a whorehouse."

I stopped dead in my tracks, turning to face my father, my vision narrowed. All I could see were his dishonest eyes.

"Well, you deserve to be in jail," I said simply, and we kept walking.

We were silent until we reached Arrow's Range Rover and exited the hotel parking lot.

Silas, who was sharing the back seat with me, took my hand. "I'm so sorry, Roxy. That was a really fucked up thing for your father to say."

I squeezed his fingers back in thanks, but could only look out the car window with my forehead leaning against the cool glass.

I was a whore? Was that what everyone was going to think if they found out I was with Arrow, Silas, and Baird?

Did people think Jessa and Birdie were whores, too, because they had unconventional relationships?

I might be stupid, but I hadn't anticipated that.

I texted Jessa.

Can you meet me at the dorm? I need to talk.

She answered immediately.

On my way.

"Looking forward to your celebration dinner?" Baird asked from the front seat.

Some celebration. Sure, I'd quit my hotel maid job, but I'd also run into my criminal father, who told me I was a whore.

I wasn't feeling very celebratory.

I leaned over the front seat and tapped Arrow on the shoulder. "Would you mind just taking me to my dorm? I… am getting a headache. I want to go home. We'll go out another night."

I felt shitty for a moment for letting the guys down, then changed my mind. If I wasn't up for socializing, I didn't have to apologize for that.

"Are you sure you want to be alone, sweetie?" Silas asked when we pulled up to the dorm.

When I nodded, he kissed my temple and let me slide out of the SUV. The guys waited for me to get inside the door, and slowly drove away.

How do I know this?

I peeked through the window, my eyes filling with tears and my throat choking with sadness. As soon as I pushed the dorm room door open, I spotted Jessa sitting there, perched on the edge of her bed, tapping her foot. The second she saw me, she jumped to her feet, and when the expression on my face registered for her, she held out her arms.

I ran into them and we hugged hard, Jessa stroking my hair and whispering in my ear.

"Tell me what happened, honey. Tell me everything."

18

SILAS FOX

AFTER DROPPING Roxy at her dorm, Arrow turned the car in the direction of home. We'd all pretty much lost our appetites, like Roxy had, and just wanted to go home, have a beer, and be mellow.

I couldn't speak for the other guys, and I didn't bring it up because I didn't want to sound like a whiny bitch, but I was getting the feeling we were moving further and further away from our plan to support Roxy. It was easy to see how that comment from her dick of a father had thrown her for a loop, and I wouldn't be surprised if he hadn't ruined it for us all.

No girl wants to be called a 'whore' by her father, even when he is a freaking wanted criminal.

I didn't want to see my girl called a whore, either, and if he hadn't been her father, I would have belted the man in the mouth.

Maybe I should have anyway. He'd screwed me and

lots of other people over by fucking up the theater renovation project. He could go to hell.

It was crazy, the impact our families had on us. I mean, the man had let his daughter down in so many ways, and yet his words still burned her to the core. I would have felt the same in her shoes.

But I wasn't her, and I was pissed. Pissed that he passed judgment on a situation he knew nothing about. Shit, when she was down and out, who took her in? Who made sure her car was running and she had phone service? Who treated her with respect?

He sure as hell hadn't.

"Can't believe I thought Roxy's dad was a hotel employee," Baird said, shaking his head where he sat in the passenger seat.

I laughed. I couldn't help it. "Talk about a classic way of sticking your foot in your mouth. But to your credit, with the way he was dressed, he did look like someone in maintenance or something. I just can't believe that's the guy responsible for single-handedly messing up the movie theater project, as well as a slew of other things."

I kind of wished we'd had the chance to bring it up. Let him know how he hadn't fucked us up as much as he had the families waiting to move into the building.

Really make the man feel like shit, was what I would have liked to do. Although he was probably already stewing in so much misery, what would have been the point aside from just trying to make ourselves feel a little better?

That said, I really wanted to find out what was going on inside his head.

"Hey guys, I'd kind of like to have a chat with our friend, Mr. Vandenberg," I said as we pulled into Arrow's driveway.

Baird chuckled. "Yeah, *no*. I've seen what you do when you need to 'have chats' with people."

Figured he'd bring that up.

"Hey, that was *one time*. And that guy really was harassing that woman. We got her out of a serious bind," I protested.

With the car stopped, Arrow looked at me in his rear-view mirror. "We did, and you're lucky he didn't press charges."

It wasn't the time to rehash that incident.

"Look guys, this is what I'm thinking. And it involves no violent confrontation, so relax. I'm wondering if there's some way we can help the man," I said.

"Help him *how*?" Arrow asked.

"Well, to begin with, he needs to drop this hiding out bit. He won't get away with it, and the longer he drags it out, the worse it will be for him. I think he's just panicked and not seeing straight. I say let's go back over there and talk to him."

The car was silent for a moment. Arrow didn't start the engine up again, but no one exited it, either.

The bottom line was, I didn't really care what happened to Roxy's father. But I did care about how his actions impacted her. We were committed to her happiness, no matter how the long-term played out, and if getting her dad back on the right path was something we could effect, then why not?

Arrow started the car back up. "How do you think we should approach this?"

"It might be better if one of us does the talking. He's gonna be on the defensive," I said.

Baird looked over his shoulder. "I suppose you're thinking you're the one who should do the talking?"

I could see neither of them was fully sold on the idea. But at least they hadn't dismissed it outright.

"I'll volunteer but if one of you wants to step up, go for it."

Arrow shook his head. "It's all yours, man."

Truth be told, Arrow was the most level-headed among us, and would probably be the best to represent us in any adversarial situation. But, he'd ceded this one to me.

Which I was fine with.

Roxy's dad had backed himself in a corner. A terrible corner from which there was no coming back. He just didn't realize it yet. But he would.

And that might bring some closure to our girl.

Fuck yeah, I was smitten by her.

"He said he's a *guest* at the hotel. Thought that was interesting," Baird said.

I could only imagine how he was 'paying for it.' Possibly with the money he'd stolen from his company, which was earmarked for the movie theater project?

Or maybe just with bad credit cards? I guess once you're so down in the shit, you'll try anything.

Arrow pulled into the busy circular drive in front of the hotel where bellmen were carrying bags and directing traffic. He tossed the keys to a valet. "We'll be back in ten minutes," he told the young guy, who nodded.

But as soon as we entered the lobby, we realized our visit was going to be *very* brief.

The police had gotten to Mr. Vandenberg before we had.

Probably for the best. I mean, that was the desired outcome, in any case.

From a distance, we watched Roxy's father try to reason with the cops, as well as the hotel manager, who'd presumably called the police on him.

All to no avail.

He was a persistent fucker.

We watched as he was escorted out of the hotel and into an unmarked police car, one we'd just walked by, unnoticed, on our way in.

While a few heads turned to see what was going on, it was clear the hotel wanted to keep things as serene as possible. Most people in the lobby had no idea anything was going on.

But because we'd gone in there looking for Vanden-berg, we'd spotted him right off the bat.

He hung his head low as the plainclothes cops led him out in handcuffs. It was the end of the man's grift, and the beginning of a whole new set of problems. I felt for the guy. He was pretty much fucked. Of course, it was his own doing.

When we were back in the Range Rover, we were solemn. What we'd just witnessed was not a happy thing to see.

Then, I realized what we needed to do next. We didn't have much time. "Guys. We gotta let Roxy know. She can't find out from the news. Or social media."

Arrow started driving. "Shit. You're right. Text her that we're coming to pick her up so we can tell her in person. Should we take her to the house?"

I'd been wondering that too, but under the circumstances, it felt like a neutral place to talk would be more appropriate.

"I know," Arrow said. "Tell her to meet us in my classroom. No one will be there, and at this hour the building will be completely deserted and quiet."

I don't know how neutral that was, but it was a start.

We waited in the empty classroom forever, it felt like. It had probably only been twenty minutes, but it seemed like an eternity. Baird sat in a chair in the first row, playing some noisy game on his phone. Arrow was up at the white board, working out some math problem. And I just paced the room, too distracted to do anything else.

But when the door clicked open, we all stopped what we were doing.

It was our Roxy, looking fresh and beautiful like she always did—without even trying. Her ripped skinny jeans, the down puffer we'd bought her, and her red Converse sneakers were strangely perfect. Another time, I might not have taken a second look at a woman who dressed like she did.

But this was now, and Roxy was the object of my affection, no matter how unexpected that was.

Which made my decision about whether or not to leave the university a hell of a lot more complicated.

But, first things first.

"Hey, darlin'," I said, throwing my arms around her since I'd reached her first.

She clung to me, which I took as a good sign. I didn't know for certain what her thoughts were about her future with us guys, but she was letting me comfort her.

After Arrow embraced her, he left her with a kiss on the cheek, and Baird took her by the hand and led her to a chair.

"Please sit down, Roxy," he said.

She furrowed her brow, looking from one of us to the other, but did as asked.

Gripping the edge of the desk so hard her knuckles were white, she paled when she realized how serious we were.

Baird crouched down in front of her. "Roxy. I'm gonna get right to the point. We were just at the hotel.

Your father's been arrested. He was escorted out by police."

Her hand flew to her mouth. I guess no matter how prepared you are for certain news, when it finally comes, it can still knock you flat.

"Are you sure?" she asked in a quiet voice, her shoulders slumped.

Baird nodded.

Roxy sighed deeply as a couple big tears rolled down her cheeks. She wiped them away as fast as they'd appeared.

"We wanted to tell you before you heard it some other way," I added.

She nodded. "Thank you. I appreciate it."

She closed her eyes, and rolled her head around on her neck, as if to release tension. Then she let out a long breath.

"I know it's for the best, but thinking of my dad in jail… well, it hurts. It really does."

We were silent, waiting for her to process everything.

"I just don't know how he got so off track. I mean, he had everything. He really did. Our family was happy. We weren't well off, but we made it work."

"People make mistakes, darlin'. And sometimes we have no idea why," I said. "Sometimes *they* have no idea why."

She nodded, and I could swear the resignation on her face was slowly turning to relief. "It's good news, actually. I know that sounds strange, but now things will start to be put right."

I loved her strength.

Arrow walked over and pulled her to her feet. "That's the perfect way to look at it, baby. I'm proud of you. We all are."

A second later, he was kissing her deeply, and she was kissing him back, having fallen right into his arms, her preoccupations of a moment earlier swept aside by his caring.

Without a sound, I walked over to the classroom door, and pressed the lock button.

You know, just in case.

Arrow backed her up to the large desk at the front of the room, lifted her ass, and set her down on it. He continued kissing her while unbuttoning her blouse. As soon as her breasts were bared, he started kissing one, and Baird stepped in to play with the other.

Roxy leaned back with one hand on the desk, her other pulling Baird closer. Catching my gaze over his head, she motioned me over with her chin, a sly smile indicating what she had in mind.

"C'mon Silas," she said.

As soon as I got close enough, Baird and Arrow made way for me. Roxy jumped off the desk and, pointing with a finger, indicated for me to take the place where she'd been sitting. Who was I to argue?

To my delight, she made quick work of my jeans and boxers, and as soon as they were down around my ankles, I kicked them off so I could move. She zeroed in on my aching erection, pushing my legs apart for maximum access.

After running her tongue around my cockhead and slurping up my precum, she lowered her mouth on me until I hit the back of her throat. The sensation nearly made me jump out of my skin, it was so sweet, and it was all I could do to hold my explosion.

With her bent over in front of me, Baird lowered her jeans below her ass and started rubbing his cock between her pretty ass cheeks.

Our girl was being tag-teamed again, and she was so excited, she ground back against Baird's face, and sucked me so hard I pounded the desk where I was sitting.

Arrow, in the meantime, reached under her, and from the way she moaned on my cock, I knew he was giving her clit the special treatment she so loved.

Watching the whole scene was enough to drive any man crazy. Especially me.

I knew I wouldn't hold out for long, which was fine because I was sure Roxy wanted to enjoy all of us.

"Baby, take my balls. Grab them, please," I said.

Her fingers eagerly grasped my sac, now throbbing with a mounting orgasm. "Yeah, baby, not too hard. Yes, like that. A little more," I growled.

"Oh fuck!" I hollered, hoping no one was in the building besides janitorial staff, who were usually discreet.

I exploded into Roxy's mouth, and she sucked every drop of my cum like a fucking champ. And before she could even wipe the dribble from her chin, Baird jumped up on the desk, lain back, and pulled her onto his sheathed cock.

I staggered to my feet, my head spinning, but not about to miss our girl taking her first dick of the day.

Yup. The first. It wouldn't be the last. I was goddamn sure of that.

Arrow and I positioned ourselves behind Roxy's ass and watched her glistening pussy lips part to accept Baird.

At first, he entered her just enough to open her up. She groaned at the stretch, but then began to bounce her ass in the air, taking more and more of him until he was halfway inside. From behind, Arrow reached between her legs, parted her lips further with his thumbs, and watched her engulf Baird until there was nothing left of him to see except his balls.

Holy fuck. I didn't think I'd ever seen anything quite so hot. As Baird slipped in and out of her silky pussy, Arrow continued playing with her, taking some moisture and rubbing it on her asshole.

We knew what was next, because we knew Arrow. He might look all straight and buttoned up on the outside, but he was an ass man if ever there was one. Without hesitation, he inched one and then two fingers up her pretty asshole.

"Fuck," Baird yelled. "She just got twice as tight on me. Oh fuck, she's milking my cock," he said, grabbing her hips and bouncing her on his dick.

Arrow followed his rhythm and eventually had his

two fingers all the way up her bum. She bucked, blonde hair flying all over, and in between gasping for breath, screamed with pleasure.

I'd just come, but damn if I wasn't already hard again watching our girl get railed on the desk in the front of a classroom. I stroked my dick as I watched the scene before me play out, wondering if Roxy was about to get her first DP.

That's when Arrow climbed up onto the desk behind Roxy, and spitting on his dick, positioned it against her pink asshole where his fingers had just been. While Baird continued sliding in and out from under her, Arrow pressed into her ass.

She groaned and Arrow leaned forward, next to her ear. "Push out baby, it will go in easier."

She closed her eyes, and I watched Arrow slide in her ass, her pussy already full of Baird.

Holy fuck. Our girl was hot, but I'd never thought she was a DP kind of woman.

Arrow gently pulsed inside her, not pushing further in but not pulling out, either. "You good baby, you like two dicks?" he growled.

She sure as hell looked like she liked two dicks.

"Mmmm," was all she could say. She nodded and with one hand gripping Baird's shoulder in front of her, she reached behind herself and pulled Arrow deeper.

"You sure, baby?" he asked. "You sure you can take more?"

"Ugghhhh."

Arrow pushed a little further inside, and that's when Roxy exploded in orgasm, throwing her hair around and screaming.

"I'm gonna come too," Baird yelled breathlessly, and with a final thrust, held himself deep inside Roxy while he spasmed beneath her.

Arrow gently pulsed in her ass and with a loud groan, popped out of her behind, stroking himself until he spurted all over her. His cum dribbled down between her crack, to her pussy, and to the desk below.

I didn't know who was going to be using this classroom next, but I hoped they never found out what had happened on top of that desk.

19

ROXY VANDENBERG

"I'll wait out here in the car. I have lots of studying to do, so just take your time."

I reached across the front seat and threw my arms around my dear friend Jessa. I didn't know what I'd do without her.

With my backpack thrown over one shoulder, I squared myself, lifted my chin up, and headed for the front doors of the county jail.

My dad's new home. At least for a while.

What a whirlwind the last twenty-four hours had been. And I'd thought the last few weeks of my life had been crazy.

The most important thing—or maybe *one* of the most important things—was that Dad was finally arrested.

Now, no daughter wants to see her dad behind bars. I certainly didn't. But I considered it a new level of maturity for myself, accepting that it was where he needed to be, at least for the time being, while he made amends to the people he hurt. I mean, yeah, the law was pretty much forcing him to do that, but I'd take what I could get.

I was so happy I was no longer employed by the hotel, which he'd ripped off like so many others in his wake.

Unbelievably, Arrow had offered to pay his hotel bill. I'd said no. It was only the tip of the iceberg with regard to Dad's debts, and if I let him pay this one, god knew where or when he'd stop. Yes, Dad's grift had been that far-reaching.

And now I was here to visit him.

Jessa and Birdie had asked me if it was a good idea. After all, my being called a whore by my father didn't sit well with them, especially since they'd found love with more than one professor, themselves. They'd seen it as a personal affront to their chosen lifestyles, and were understandably combative about it, as well as defensive of me.

"You do not deserve to be spoken to that way."

"He's a fine one to pass judgment, after all he's done."

Their indignation continued until I cut it off.

The night they'd met me in their dorm room, when I'd blown off dinner with the guys, I waved at them both like a *stop* sign.

"Thanks, guys. I so appreciate your support. But, I can't help but ask myself whether going forward with the guys' proposal is a good idea."

Jessa sat back and looked at me hard. "Okay. Let's start here then. How attached to them are you? The guys?"

I hadn't thought much about that.

Actually, it wasn't that I hadn't thought about it, it was just that I'd purposely tried *not* to think about it, period.

Because, after all, how much I liked the guys was immaterial when the likelihood of a successful relationship between us was the more pressing matter. I could like Arrow, Baird, and Silas all I wanted, but if we couldn't be together, that was the end of that.

And with each passing moment it seemed more likely that's how things were going to turn out, especially if my father, who had historically always been on my side, thought I was a whore.

Others were sure to think even worse, right?

Like Paloma.

Although her perspective was colored by the fact that she'd had the hots for Arrow, and her admiration had never gotten her any closer to him. It was hard for a girl for whom the seas parted when she so commanded, to be overlooked by someone like him.

Not that that was my problem.

But if Dad had spewed such vitriol at my situation, wouldn't everyone else do the same?

Birdie and Jessa disagreed.

Their experience had not borne such a negative reaction.

Besides, Birdie had pointed out, why did I give a shit about what other people thought, anyway?

It was a legit question.

I put my things through the county jail X-ray machine and walked through the metal detector once inside. After some paperwork and several locked doors, I was face-to-face with my father through a thick glass window. He wore a jumpsuit that was several sizes too large, and his hands were cuffed in front of him, attached to a chain belt around his waist.

I grabbed my seat before I stumbled. No matter what the man had done, it was still shocking to see him like this. In fact, it pretty much broke my heart, seeing someone I'd always looked up to, fall so, so far. When I pushed my anger aside for a moment, I realized just how much I was shaken by his actions. I knew he hadn't done anything directly to me, per se, but I couldn't deny the devastating betrayal, anyway.

"Hello, Roxy," he said, looking like he'd aged ten years since I'd seen him. "You just missed your mother."

"Yes, Mom told me she was coming to visit. Did Niki come, too?" I asked.

Dad shook his head. "No. Your sister's too young to visit. I don't want her to see me here."

Didn't blame him.

"Mom's still staying at your aunt's house. She seems to be doing okay," he said.

Wishful thinking, Dad.

I wasn't going to tell him how he'd fucked over Mom. I was sure she'd done a good job of that, herself.

I was there for *me.*

"Dad, I wanted to come and tell you that you don't get to judge me for the way I solve a problem that you caused for me."

His eyes narrowed. "Are you talking about those guys you were with?"

I nodded. "Yes. They are… friends. And they've given me work that will help pay for my tuition, so I don't have to drop out of school."

He didn't need to know any more than that, including the guys' longer-term proposal, and that it included living with them. And other things.

Dad looked around, not that there was much to look at, and started moving his cuffed hands to get more comfortable when he remembered they were chained to his waist. I caught sigh of my dad's familiar, callused hands. It was a punch to the gut.

"I… I'm sorry," he said, finally looking at me.

The sadness in his eyes was overwhelming. I had to get out of there.

"I forgive you, Dad," I said, and got up to leave.

I really did forgive him. And it felt great.

"How'd it go?" Jessa asked, closing the big text book she'd been highlighting while waiting for me in the car.

I pulled on my seatbelt, and stared ahead. I was numb and at a loss for words.

Jessa reached for my hand and squeezed it. "I'm sorry you're going through this, sweetie. It's been such a shit time."

She started her car, and we drove away from the jail. And my dad. And, I hoped, a lot of what had been plaguing me.

"You know Jessa, it has been a shitstorm of craziness. But like you always say, something good comes out of every disaster."

She glanced at me as she steered us back toward campus. "Oh yeah? Tell me."

"If this hadn't all happened, I don't know that I'd really have gotten to know the guys. I mean, I knew Baird as my academic advisor and Arrow as my finance teacher, but that would have been the extent of it. And I never would have met Silas at all."

She laughed. "Are you saying what I think you're saying?"

As she pulled onto the freeway, I looked out the passenger side window at the scenery whizzing by. "Maybe."

And we both burst out laughing.

2 0

BAIRD PRIESTLY

"Is this everything?"

Roxy nodded. I think it was a point of pride with her, how few belongings she owned.

Another thing I loved about her.

Yes, I said *loved*.

Although I'd not told her that. Yet.

I followed her friends Jessa and Birdie as they carried the last of Roxy's clothing, which she'd stuffed into a couple oversized duffels, to the guest room.

Which was her new room.

Yup, she'd decided to move in with us and make a go of our proposal. I mean, she'd already been working for us, but she finally came clean and shared that she had feelings for the three of us guys. To say we were happy to hear the news was an understatement.

I think it might have had something to do with the crazy sexy session we'd had in the classroom. The guys didn't think that swayed her either way, but I thought they were idiots.

Of course, it had. She liked getting fucked by three guys. As long as the guys were Arrow, Silas, and me.

She walked her girlfriends to the door. "Thanks so much for helping, ladies. I love you both."

Of course, Roxy had spent the night over our house before, many times in fact, but there was something much more permanent about having your friends help you move. It sort of sealed the deal, as if they were giving their blessing. Figuratively carrying her over the threshold.

And how could they not be happy for her? They each had their own student/professor romance thing going on.

Smart girls.

If you'd asked me at the beginning of the semester, when Roxy came to me in a panic, whether we'd be doing what we are now, I would have laughed my ass off.

Me with a student?

Arrow and Silas with a student?

There was just no way.

And yet here we were. One big, happy family.

Silas cooked us all a big steak dinner, and after Roxy's friends left, I went upstairs to run her a hot bath. We lit candles and brought champagne, and watched our beautiful girl lower herself into an over-sized, clawfoot tub.

"What's all this for?" she asked, laughing and taking a sip of her bubbly.

"It's a celebration," I said.

She looked at each of us. "Of anything in particular?"

Arrow shrugged. "Yeah. So much. We're proud of you, baby. You've come out on top. You're on track to accomplish everything you want."

Her lip quivered, like I'd suspected it might. She might come off as a tough chick, but her vulnerable side was always right there, just below the surface. "You guys," she said. "None of this would have happened if not for you."

Silas shook his head. "I don't know I'd say that, darlin'. Sure, we presented you some opportunities, but you're the one who put them into action. There's only so far we could take you."

It was true. Now that Roxy was back on track, she'd finish school in another year since she could focus on taking classes, rather than taking shifts as a hotel maid. And the 'work' she was doing for us guys? Well, if we needed her help for something, we let her know. But we really just wanted her to focus on her studies.

There'd be plenty of time for jobs after graduation.

"But, pretty girl, you are not the only thing we're celebrating tonight," Arrow added.

"Oh really?" she asked, her free hand disappearing under the water.

Shit. I knew what she was doing, damn her. I had some work to do tonight, and it was becoming clear that I—and the other guys—were about to be occupied by something much more fun.

"I've…" Silas started to say, "decided to leave the university. I'm taking the job with the architectural firm."

The smile on Roxy's face withered. And for good reason.

Her hand shook, sloshing champagne out of her glass. "You're leaving town?" she asked in a cracking voice.

Silas smiled. "Actually, *no*. I've arranged so I can do my work from here. I'll have to travel to the office once a month, and of course meet with clients, but my home base will be here."

Relief washed over her face and her smile returned. "Oh my god. You gave me a heart attack for a moment there," she laughed.

Silas sat on the edge of the bathtub and leaned down to kiss her on the forehead. "Sorry, babe."

"So that means you'll be finishing your house here?" she asked.

He beamed with pride. "Oh yes. Definitely, yes."

I'd seen the plans. The place was going to be freaking awesome. In fact, he'd asked if Arrow and I wanted to move over to his place. Nothing was decided yet, but it was nice to have options. Besides, I figured anything we ended up doing would be influenced by whatever preference Roxy had.

I couldn't lie. I knew she'd be calling the shots eventually. Even without meaning to, she had us three pretty much wrapped around her finger.

'Course, she was wrapped around ours, too. And other things.

Roxy stood in the tub, rivers of water running down her skin, now was exploding in goosebumps.

I grabbed a towel and began rubbing her down with it. Arrow took one of her hands, and helped her out of the tub. She stood, naked and beautiful, her long wet hair clinging to her shoulders and breasts like a mermaid. She stepped off the bathmat, and beckoned us with a finger. No questions asked, we silently followed her.

When we got to her bedroom, she turned to face us. "This is everything I ever wanted and more. Thank you so much," she whispered, kissing each of us as we laid her back on the bed.

EPILOGUE

My dad ended up going to prison for several years, but with good behavior, I was told he might get out early. He started up construction management classes for his fellow prisoners, so that's earning him major points and keeping him busy. He told me he's happy to have a chance to make some restitution after screwing up so royally.

I still don't really understand how someone like my dad

could get so far off track. It was like he temporarily lost his mind, and all ability to use good judgment. Even his calling me a... well, I couldn't repeat it, but that wasn't like him, either. And boy had he apologized for it. He hadn't seen the guys since that one time in the hotel, but Mom had, and while she didn't 'get' our relationship, I think she was just glad to have something positive happening in her world. It was a load off her shoulders that they were helping me with school, but more importantly that I'd hooked up with decent, kind men who had integrity. I knew when she looked at them, she compared them to Dad, which was a mistake. She was only going to make herself unhappy doing that. At least until he proved he was worthy of her trust, which would take a long time, if it ever happened.

It's weird, having a dad behind bars. It kind of shakes up all you think you know about the world, not to mention your identity. I know I didn't commit the crimes, but who doesn't feel that their family is a reflection on themselves, and vice versa?

I believed that for a long time. But no more. I'm not the criminal. Dad is. I've had to look at myself through a new and different lens, which was pretty much made possible by the guys—Baird, Arrow, and Silas. If I hadn't had their support while going through the shit show I did, I'm not sure what would have become of me.

Actually, that's a lie. I would have figured it out. Come out on top. Somehow. Even if it killed me. But it was a hell of a lot more enjoyable with three gorgeous, accomplished men having my back. And other parts.

I was able to finish my semester as a real, live enrolled student, thanks to Arrow's taking over my tuition. We got my bills straightened out and I formally enrolled just in time to earn credit for the semester. And, thanks to the guys, I got all A's and B's.

Okay, well I got one A and the rest B's. But I'm not complaining. It felt good to finally have a report card without a single C on it, not even in that god-awful calculus class. That was a new thing for me and a good excuse for a celebration.

As if we ever needed a reason to celebrate.

Now that I'm living in Arrow's house pretty much full-time, I frequently see Paloma, my bitchy down-the-street neighbor. What's different is that I no longer feel compelled to be sneaky every time I come and go. So, when I see her, I wave and smile, sure to display just how close the guys and I have become, whether it's by holding hands or out-and-out kissing right there in the middle of the driveway.

She hasn't bothered me since. In fact last time I saw her, I'm pretty sure she just looked straight ahead as she drove past, despite my obvious hand wave.

I'd mentioned her one time to Arrow, wondering if he knew of her infatuation with him.

"Paloma who?" he asked. "Is she in one of my classes?"

Enough said.

My mom and little sister are still staying with my aunt. Mom got a job at the university as a secretary in the president's office. We all had great benefits now, and more security than we'd had in years. And because of Arrow's generosity regarding my tuition, I gave the money I'd saved from my maid job straight to Mom. But old habits die hard. The guys had to keep reminding me to stop cleaning the house. But I couldn't. I just liked things at the level of tidiness I'd learned from my years working at the hotel. It felt good to pitch in.

And it felt so good to know I was staying in school and that nothing could get in my way again. Arrow said he could introduce me to his Wall Street cronies from back in the day when I got closer to graduation, if I wanted to pursue a career path like that. I had to admit, I loved the idea of being a hard-charging finance chick kicking ass in the Big Apple and making a shit ton of money, but it probably meant I'd have to leave town. That was a hard no. I wasn't giving up my guys.

I mean, shit, would you, if you were me?

So with that in mind, who the hell knew what I'd do when I finished school. But I had options, yo.

Speaking of options, Silas decided to stay with the university. Yes, he did. At the eleventh hour he announced that as cool as it would be to work on retail spaces, he just couldn't leave Wellshire. He loved teaching. But he was in the process of setting up a pro-bono program for the school, where local projects like the movie theater would be designed by student architects—of course with his oversight. With this, he'd be able to keep his fingers in both worlds, which turned out to be the perfect combination for him.

Rather than wait for the construction firm my father had left in financial straits to get back on its feet, Baird had somehow, miraculously, managed to raise enough money to keep the movie theater renovation moving forward. After a while, I stopped feeling sick to my stomach with guilt every time I heard the project mentioned, and was able to share his joy in having contributed something so meaningful to the town. In fact, with the influx of new funds, the project was finished in double time. When we attended the grand opening, with my three guys up on the dais, beaming alongside the families that would be housed in the building, I couldn't stop crying. I was so proud of them, and happy for the families that would have stable housing. I knew what it was like to almost not have a roof over my head. I couldn't imagine what it would be like to live with a fear like that every day, and not have friends to fall back on.

My friends were everything to me, and I finally got Arrow to tell me the whole story of how he lost a friend a while back, something he'd alluded to a couple times but never completely shared. Seems there was a college scholarship for which he and his best buddy had competed. Arrow got it, and that was the end of their friendship. He'd been grieving about it ever since. It made me sad to hear, especially since he couldn't see a way through to a remedy. Those are the cards life deals you sometimes, he'd told me.

My friends, on the other hand, couldn't be happier with their lives, and the hot professors who were part of them.

Birdie, who'd magically ended up with a monopoly on the hot teachers in the English department, had collaborated with her guys on a screenplay based on a book Leo had written long ago, which had enjoyed a resurgence of popularity to the point where Hollywood had noticed. She promised that when the movie was all said and done, and it was time for the premier, that we'd all head out to California *together and get a fabulous house on the beach in Malibu for the occasion.*

I couldn't believe it. How had I gone from essentially living on the wrong side of the tracks, even referred to as a townie by certain assholes, to going to a Hollywood premier and crashing on the beach in a cool house in Malibu? I guess my griping about the universe shitting all over me had earned me a break or two or three. I felt so lucky. I was so lucky.

My other bestie, Jessa, was well on her way to making a name for herself in the art world thanks to her massive talent and commitment to the work. Sure, her guys had her back through everything, but she'd made it all happen on her own through sheer tenacity. She'd gotten into that art show and won the prize scholarship, which had not only given her the independence to scoot out from under her parents' expectations but also give her visibility that just wouldn't have come any other way. I was so proud of her. Silas had an eye on one of her paintings for his house, which was nearly complete. I was looking forward to being able to see her talent hanging on our walls every day.

Our walls. It felt good to say that. As soon as Silas's house was complete, we'd all be moving over there. The place was massive, and we'd always be able to spread out for alone time when needed, and together time... hopefully a lot. Like every night.

Maybe we were still in the honeymoon phase, where we couldn't get enough of each other. But I had a strong suspicion I would always be head over heels with my guys, excited about waking up with them every morning, and going to sleep with them every night.

BONUS EXTENDED EPILOGUE...

What happens next with Roxy and her three hot men?
Check out this BONUS Extended Epilogue

I hope you loved reading this book as much as I loved writing it. Please visit my store to learn more about my books, and to buy directly from me! https://mikalaneshop.com/

Dear Reader:

I'm USA TODAY bestselling romance author Mika Lane, and am OBSESSED with bringing you sassy, steamy stories with imperfect heroines and the bad-a*s dudes they bring to their knees. I'll always bring you my signature humor and heat, topped off with a modern-day happily ever after.

My first book ever was *The Day I Ate the Milkyway*, a true fourth-grade masterpiece illustrated with crayons and bound with construction paper and glue. Nowadays, steamy romance gives purpose to my days and nights as I create worlds and characters that tickle the imagination. I live in magical Northern California with my own handsome alpha dude, sometimes known as Mr. Mika Lane, and two devilish cats named Chuck and Murray.

A dual citizen of the United States and Ireland, I have on more than one occasion spent my last dollar on a plane ticket somewhere, and am always planning my next escape. I often try new recipes on unsuspecting friends, search out hiding places to read undisturbed, and sadly kill every houseplant I bring home.

I LOVE to hear from readers when I'm not dreaming up naughty tales to share. Visit my online shop https:// mikalaneshop.com/ and say hello https:// mikalaneshop.com/pages/meet-mika.

xoxo, Mika